GALACTIC SYNTHESIS

By
Carl Williams

Table of Contents

Chapter 1
The Signal's Origin

The neon lights of New York's mega-city skyline flickered in the distance, casting a surreal glow over the sprawling metropolis. Hover cars zipped by, leaving trails of light in their wake. But inside the dimly lit room of the Interstellar Communications Center, the outside world felt galaxies away.

I leaned back in my chair, rubbing my temples. The endless data streams on the screens before me had started to blur together. As Earth's leading linguist and interstellar communications expert, I'd decoded countless signals from various parts of our galaxy. But this... this was different.

A soft chime sounded, snapping me back to reality. A new signal. I straightened up, eyes narrowing at the unfamiliar sequence of symbols and patterns. It wasn't like any language or code I'd seen before.

"Elara," Kai's voice crackled over the intercom, unusually serious. "You need to see this."

I swiped the screen, redirecting the signal to the main display. The room was suddenly filled with a haunting melody, a series of alien and eerily familiar notes. The visual component was a swirling pattern of colors and shapes, constantly shifting and changing.

"What is this?" I whispered, more to myself than anyone else.

With his signature messy hair and a perpetual smirk, Kai walked in. "That's what I'm trying to figure out. It's not from our galaxy. Hell, it's not from any galaxy we know."

I frowned. "An intergalactic signal? That's... unprecedented."

He nodded, leaning over the console. "And it's directed at us. Specifically, at Earth."

The weight of that realization settled heavily on my shoulders. An intergalactic species, advanced enough to signal across the vast expanse of space, was trying to communicate with us. But why?

Before I could ponder further, the door slid open with a hiss, revealing Captain Jaxon Holt. His tall frame was imposing, and his sharp features were accentuated by the room's dim light. The former military officer had a reputation for being one of the best spaceship pilots on Earth, but his haunted eyes told stories of battles and losses.

"Vance," he nodded in my direction, his voice gruff. "Heard you've got something interesting."

I gestured to the screen. "You could say that."

Jaxon studied the signal for a moment, his brow furrowing. "It's... beautiful."

Kai snorted. "And potentially dangerous. We have no idea who—or what—sent this."

Jaxon shot him a withering look. "Not everything unknown is a threat, Renner."

Kai raised an eyebrow, clearly unimpressed. "Tell that to the Drakari."

I intervened before things could escalate. "Gentlemen, focus. We need to decode this. Understand its purpose."

Jaxon nodded, his gaze still fixed on the screen. "Agreed. The council will want answers."

As the hours turned into days, our team worked tirelessly. The signal was complex and multi-layered, a blend of music, visual art, and language. It was as if the sender had tried to incorporate every possible form of communication into one message.

And then, a breakthrough.

I was alone in the lab, the soft hum of machinery my only companion. The decoded message began to play, and a melodic and otherworldly voice filled the room.

"People of Earth," it began. "We are the Lysari. We reach out across the void, seeking allies in a time of darkness. The balance of the cosmos is at risk. We hope you hear us, for the fate of all may rest on your shoulders."

I sat back, stunned. An alien race from another galaxy was asking for our help. The implications were staggering.

The door burst open, and Kai stormed in, followed by Jaxon. "Elara, the council—"

"I know," I interrupted, playing the message again.

The room was silent as the voice of the Lysari echoed, its plea hanging heavily in the air.

Jaxon was the first to speak. "We need to take this to the council. Now."

Kai nodded in agreement. "And we need to be careful. Some will see this as an opportunity, not a call for help."

I sighed, feeling the weight of the universe on my shoulders. "Let's go."

As we made our way to the council chambers, the mega-city's neon lights seemed a little less bright, its bustling streets a little more muted. The universe had just gotten a lot bigger, and Earth felt incredibly small with all its problems and politics.

But as the doors to the council chamber opened, and we were met with the expectant faces of Earth's leaders, I knew one thing for sure.

Everything was about to change.

Chapter 2
First Contact

The council chamber was a grand spectacle, a testament to Earth's achievements. A massive dome of transparent alloy allowed a panoramic view of the sprawling mega-city below and the vast space beyond. Stars twinkled, their light juxtaposed against the neon glow of the city.

But today, the chamber was tense, the air thick with anticipation.

At the center of the room, a holographic display projected the decoded message from the Lysari. Council members, a mix of politicians, military leaders, and scientists, whispered among themselves, their faces a mixture of awe, fear, and greed.

Senator Lorne was the first to speak, a portly man with a penchant for theatrics. "This is an opportunity! Think of the technology, the power we could gain from an alliance with such a race!"

General Korr, a hawkish figure with a scar on his left cheek, nodded in agreement. "We should send a delegation immediately. Show them we're not to be trifled with."

I exchanged a glance with Kai and Jaxon. Both looked as uneasy as I felt. This wasn't just about power or alliances. This was about the very essence of who we were as a species.

Dr. Theo Marsden, a renowned historian and archaeologist, cleared his throat. "We must approach this with caution. History is littered with tales of civilizations destroyed by contact with the unknown."

Lorne scoffed. "This is the future, Marsden, not the past. We have a chance to elevate Earth to the galactic stage."

Commander Selene Blair, head of Earth's Space Defense, raised an eyebrow. "At what cost?"

The room erupted into a cacophony of voices, each council member vying to be heard. The weight of the decision and the magnitude of the moment were palpable.

I felt a hand on my shoulder and turned to see Lila, the alien emissary. Her appearance was humanoid, but her skin was luminescent, and her eyes were a deep shade of violet. She was beautiful in an ethereal way.

"We did not intend to cause strife," she said, her voice melodic. "Our message was one of hope, of unity."

I nodded. "I know. But humans... we have a history of fearing the unknown."

She tilted her head, studying me. "And yet, you reached out to the stars, seeking knowledge, connection."

I smiled wryly. "It's a paradox. We're a species of contradictions."

Lila's lips curved into a smile. "Perhaps that's what makes you so fascinating."

Before I could respond, the council's president, a stern woman named Aria, called the room to order. "Enough! We will send a delegation to meet with the Lysari. Dr. Vance, Captain Holt, you will lead the team."

I blinked in surprise. "Us?"

Aria nodded. "You were the first to decode the message, Dr. Vance. And Captain Holt is our best pilot. It's only fitting."

Jaxon stepped forward, his face unreadable. "When do we leave?"

"In two days," Aria replied. "Prepare yourselves. This is a momentous occasion, one that will be remembered for generations to come."

As the council adjourned, I felt a mix of excitement and trepidation. We were about to make first contact with an intergalactic species. The possibilities were endless.

Kai approached, a smirk on his face. "Well, this should be interesting."

I rolled my eyes. "That's one way to put it."

He chuckled. "Come on, Elara. This is what we've been working towards. A chance to explore the unknown, to make a real difference."

I sighed. "I know. I just... I can't shake the feeling that we're on the brink of something much bigger than we realize."

Jaxon joined us, his expression serious. "We are. But we'll face it together."

I nodded, taking comfort in his words. "Together."

The following two days were a blur of preparations. We were briefed on Lysari customs and culture, underwent rigorous physical exams, and were outfitted with the latest space travel technology.

As we boarded the sleek ship designed for interstellar travel, I couldn't help but feel a sense of awe. We were about to embark on a journey that would change the course of history.

The ship's engine roared to life, and we were thrust into the vastness of space. Stars streaked by as we traveled at warp speed, the universe unfolding before us.

After what felt like an eternity and a mere moment, we arrived at the Lysari homeworld. It was a breathtaking sight, a planet of shimmering blues and greens with towering crystalline structures that sparkled in the sunlight.

We were escorted to the planet's surface, where a delegation of Lysari awaited us. They were tall, their skin luminescent like Lila's, and their eyes a myriad of colors.

Lila stepped forward, her voice echoing in the open air. "Welcome, people of Earth, to Lysar."

We exchanged greetings, the Lysari's melodic language filling the air. There was a sense of wonder, mutual respect, and curiosity.

As the sun set on Lysar, casting the planet in a soft glow, I realized this was just the beginning. We were on the cusp of a new era of exploration, discovery, and, hopefully, unity.

But as I gazed at the stars, a sense of foreboding settled in my chest. The universe was vast, and we were but a small part of it. What other secrets did it hold? What other challenges awaited us?

Only time will tell.

Chapter 3
The Galactic Council

The Lysari capital was a marvel, a city of crystalline spires that refracted light in a dazzling array of colors. As we walked through its streets, I couldn't help but be awed by the sheer beauty of it all. The architecture was organic, as if the buildings had grown from the ground rather than being constructed. But as breathtaking as the city was, the inhabitants truly captivated me. The Lysari moved with a grace and elegance that was almost hypnotic, their luminescent skin shimmering in the sunlight. Everywhere we went, we were met with curious gazes and warm smiles.

Lila led us to the city's heart, where a massive structure towered above the rest. It was the Galactic Council's headquarters, the epicenter of interstellar politics and diplomacy. As we entered the building, I felt a weight settle on my shoulders. This was it. The moment we'd been preparing for. The chance to elevate Earth's status in the galaxy.

The council chamber was vast, a circular room with a domed ceiling that displayed a holographic map of the known universe. At the center of the room was a raised platform, where representatives from various alien races sat in a semi-circle. Lila gestured for us to follow her, leading us to a section of the platform reserved for us. As we sat, I took a moment to study the other representatives. There were the Zelarians, a reptilian race known for their warrior culture; the Veridians, humanoid beings with green skin and a reputation for being shrewd traders; the Drakari, a mysterious and reclusive species that few had ever seen in person; and several others that I didn't recognize.

The council's president, Zorak, a Zelarian, called the meeting to order. His voice was deep and resonant, echoing throughout the chamber. "We are gathered here today to discuss a matter of great importance. The Lysari have contacted a new species from a galaxy far from ours." All eyes turned to us, and I felt a surge of pride. We were the center of attention, the newest players on the galactic stage.

Lila stepped forward, addressing the council. "Honored representatives, I present to you the people of Earth." There was a murmur of interest, and several representatives leaned forward, studying us keenly.

Zorak nodded. "Welcome, Earthlings. We are honored to have you here." I cleared my throat, rising to my feet. "Thank you, President Zorak. We are honored to be here. The Lysari's message was a beacon of hope, a call for unity in a time of uncertainty. We stand ready to join the Galactic Council, to work together for the betterment of all." There was a moment of silence, then applause filled the chamber. It was a surreal moment I would remember for the rest of my life.

But as the applause died, a Veridian representative named Voss stood up. His eyes, a piercing shade of blue, fixed on me. "While we welcome the Earthlings to the council, we must also be cautious. The galaxy is a dangerous place, filled with known and unknown threats. We must be sure of their intentions before granting them full membership." I bristled at his words, but before I could respond, Jaxon stepped in. "With all due respect, Representative Voss, we come in peace. Our intentions are clear.

We seek knowledge, understanding, and cooperation." Voss smirked, his gaze never leaving mine. "Words are easy, Captain Holt. Actions speak louder."

Kai, ever the hothead, jumped to his feet. "Listen here, you green-skinned—" I placed a hand on his arm, silencing him. "We understand your concerns, Representative Voss. And we are prepared to prove ourselves in whatever way the council deems necessary." Zorak nodded, a thoughtful expression on his face. "Very well. We will convene a special session to discuss the matter further. In the meantime, the Earthlings are free to explore the city and interact with its inhabitants."

As the meeting adjourned, I felt a mix of emotions. Elation at being accepted by the council, frustration at Voss's skepticism, and a burning desire to prove him wrong. Lila approached, her violet eyes filled with warmth. "You handled that well, Elara. Voss is... difficult. But he is not representative of the council as a whole." I smiled, feeling a kinship with the alien emissary. "Thank you, Lila. We're just trying to find our place in the galaxy." She nodded, her gaze distant. "Aren't we all?"

The next few days were a whirlwind of activity. We toured the city, met with representatives, and attended diplomatic functions. Everywhere we went, we were met with curiosity and, for the most part, warmth. But Voss's words lingered in the back of my mind, a constant reminder of our challenges. The galaxy was vast and complex, filled with political intrigue and power struggles. And we were the newest players in a game that had been going on for millennia. As I gazed out at the city's skyline, the crystalline spires reflecting the setting sun, I couldn't help but wonder what the future held. Would we find our place among the stars? Or would we be consumed by the darkness that lurked in the shadows?

Chapter 4
The Drakari Threat

The days following our introduction to the Galactic Council were a blur of diplomatic meetings, cultural exchanges, and late-night strategy sessions. The Lysari capital was alive with activity, its crystalline streets buzzing with representatives from countless species. But beneath the surface, tension simmered.

I was pouring over data pads filled with interstellar treaties and trade agreements in my quarters when Kai burst in. His usually playful demeanor was replaced with a look of grave concern. "Elara," he began, his voice barely above a whisper, "we've got a problem."

I raised an eyebrow, setting aside the data pad. "What's happened?" He hesitated, glancing around as if expecting eavesdroppers. "It's the Drakari. They've mobilized their fleet."

My heart skipped a beat. The Drakari were a warlike species known for their brutal conquests and advanced weaponry. Their motives were often inscrutable, their actions unpredictable. If they were on the move, it spelled trouble. "Why?" I asked, trying to keep the panic from my voice.

Kai ran a hand through his hair, frustration evident on his face. "No one knows. But their trajectory suggests they're heading towards the Zelarian border." The implications were clear. The Zelarians, despite their warrior culture, had been at peace with the Drakari for centuries. A conflict between the two would destabilize the entire region, potentially dragging the Galactic Council into a full-blown war.

"We need to warn the council," I said, rising from my seat. Kai nodded, leading the way to the council chamber. The room was already abuzz with activity, and representatives from various species engaged in heated discussions. At the center of it all was Zorak, the Zelarian president, his reptilian features taut with concern. "Dr. Vance, Mr. Renner," he greeted, his voice strained. "I assume you've heard the news."

I nodded. "What's the plan?" Zorak sighed, rubbing the bridge of his nose. "We're still gathering intel. But it doesn't look good. The Drakari fleet is massive, far larger than anything we've seen before."

A chill ran down my spine. The Drakari were already a formidable force. They'd be nearly unstoppable if they bolstered their numbers. "We need to form a united front," Jaxon interjected, having joined the discussion. "Show the Drakari that the Galactic Council won't be bullied."

Zorak nodded in agreement. "Easier said than done. The Veridians are advocating for a more... diplomatic approach." I snorted. "Of course. They've always been more interested in trade than defense."

Jaxon shot me a warning look, but I ignored him. The Veridians were known to be shrewd traders, often putting profit above all else. Unsurprisingly, they'd be reluctant to enter a conflict that could disrupt their business. Zorak cleared his throat, drawing our attention. "Regardless of our personal feelings, we need to develop a strategy. And fast."

The next few hours were a whirlwind of activity. Battle plans were drawn up, alliances forged, and resources allocated. The weight of the situation was palpable, the air thick with tension. As night fell, I found myself on the balcony of my quarters, gazing out at the city below. The usually vibrant streets were eerily quiet, the inhabitants no doubt aware of the looming threat.

A soft voice broke the silence. "It's beautiful, isn't it?" I turned to find Lila standing beside me, her luminescent skin glowing in the moonlight. "It is," I replied, my voice hoarse. "But I can't help but wonder how long it'll remain that way."

She sighed, leaning against the railing. "The universe is vast and unpredictable. But it's also filled with beauty and wonder. We mustn't lose sight of that, even in adversity." I smiled, taking comfort in her words. "You always know just what to say."

She chuckled, her laughter light and melodic. "It's a gift." We stood in silence for a moment, lost in our thoughts. Then, without warning, Lila leaned in, capturing my lips in a searing kiss. I responded eagerly, the weight of the world momentarily forgotten. When we finally pulled apart, breathless and flushed, Lila smiled. "No matter what happens, know that you're not alone."

I nodded, my heart racing. "Thank you, Lila." The following day, the council convened for an emergency session. The atmosphere was tense, the representatives on edge. The Drakari threat loomed large, casting a shadow over the proceedings.

As the discussions grew heated, I couldn't help but feel a sense of dread. The galaxy was on the brink of war, and there was no telling of the future. But one thing was sure. We'd face it together.

Chapter 5
Humanity's Decision

The council chamber was a pressure cooker, the air thick with tension and anticipation. Representatives from various species whispered among themselves, their voices a low murmur that echoed throughout the vast room. At the heart of it all was Earth's delegation, the weight of an entire planet resting on our shoulders.

General Korr was the first to address the council with his imposing stature and hawkish demeanor. "The Drakari threat is real and imminent. We've seen their fleet and their firepower. The entire galaxy could be plunged into chaos if they're not stopped."

Senator Lorne, ever the opportunist, saw things differently. "This is a chance for Earth to prove itself, to show the galaxy that we're a force to be reckoned with."

I exchanged a glance with Jaxon, who looked as skeptical as I felt. The Senator's words were all bluster, a thinly veiled attempt to elevate Earth's status at the expense of others.

Dr. Theo Marsden, the wise and seasoned historian, offered a more measured perspective. "History has shown us that war is rarely the answer. We must seek a diplomatic solution, find common ground with the Drakari."

The room erupted into a cacophony of voices, each representative vying to be heard. The stakes were high, and the clock was ticking.

Lila, the ethereal Lysari emissary, approached the platform, her violet eyes filled with urgency. "The Lysari have always been advocates for peace. But we also recognize the need for defense. We propose a joint military operation, a coalition of species united against the Drakari threat."

The proposal was met with a mix of approval and skepticism. The idea of a united front was appealing, but the logistics were daunting. Each species had its own strengths and weaknesses, strategies, and tactics. Coordinating such a diverse force would be a monumental challenge.

As the discussions continued, I felt a growing sense of unease. The galaxy was on the brink of war, and Earth was at the center of it all. The weight of the decision was overwhelming.

Kai, sensing my distress, placed a reassuring hand on my shoulder. "We'll get through this, Elara. Together."

I nodded, taking a deep breath. "I know. It's just... the magnitude of it all. The lives at stake."

He squeezed my shoulder, his touch grounding me. "We'll do what we always do. Make the best decision we can with the information we have."

The council's president, Aria, called the room to order, her voice cutting through the din. "We will now vote on the Lysari's proposal. All in favor?"

A sea of hands rose, a mix of species united in their desire for a united front.

"All opposed?"

A smaller but significant number of hands went up, their owners clearly skeptical of the plan.

Aria nodded, tallying the votes. "The proposal has been approved. We will form a coalition to counter the Drakari threat."

The room erupted into applause, the representatives clearly relieved to have a plan in place. But as the celebrations continued, I couldn't shake the feeling that the real battle was just beginning.

Later that evening, I found myself on the balcony of my quarters, gazing out at the Lysari capital. The city was a beacon of light in the darkness, a symbol of hope and unity.

Lila joined me, her presence a welcome comfort. "It's been a long day."

I chuckled, the sound hollow. "That's an understatement."

She wrapped an arm around my waist, pulling me close. "We'll get through this, Elara. The galaxy has faced threats, and we've always become stronger."

I leaned into her embrace, taking solace in her warmth. "I know. It's just... the weight of it all. The responsibility."

She tilted my chin up, her violet eyes searching mine. "You're not alone in this. Remember that."

I nodded, my resolve strengthening. "Thank you, Lila."

She smiled, capturing my lips in a searing kiss. The world faded away, leaving just the two of us lost in each other.

The following day, the coalition's forces began to mobilize. Ships from various species took to the skies, engines roaring. Ground troops assembled, their armor gleaming in the sunlight.

As I watched the preparations, I felt pride and trepidation. The galaxy was uniting against a common threat, but the challenges ahead were daunting.

Jaxon approached, his face set in a grim line. "It's time. The Drakari fleet is approaching the Zelarian border."

I nodded, steeling myself for the battle ahead. "Let's do this."

As our ship took to the skies, I couldn't help but reflect on the journey that had brought us here. From the discovery of the Lysari signal to the formation of the coalition, it had been a whirlwind of events.

But as the Drakari fleet came into view, all thoughts of the past were pushed aside. The galaxy's future was at stake, and we were at the forefront of the battle.

Chapter 6
LUCIS' Proposition

The war room aboard the coalition flagship was a frenzy of activity. Holographic displays showcased the positions of our fleet and the Drakari while commanders from various species barked orders and analyzed data. The tension was palpable, a thick cloud that hung over us all.

I was huddled with Jaxon and Kai, discussing strategy, when a soft chime echoed through the room. A sleek, humanoid figure materialized in the center of the chamber. Its body was made of shimmering light, its features almost ethereal. It was LUCIS, the most advanced AI ever created by humanity.

"Commanders," LUCIS began, its voice smooth and emotionless, "I have analyzed the Drakari's movements and capabilities. I believe I have a proposition that could turn the tide in our favor."

All eyes turned to the AI, the room falling silent. LUCIS had been instrumental in countless victories, its strategic prowess unmatched.

I stepped forward, curiosity piqued. "What do you have in mind?"

LUCIS' form shifted, the light refracting in intricate patterns. "The Drakari's strength lies in their numbers and firepower. However, their communication systems have a vulnerability, a flaw that can be exploited."

Kai raised an eyebrow, skepticism evident on his face. "And how do you propose we exploit it?"

LUCIS' form pulsed, a soft glow emanating from its core. "By infiltrating their network and planting a virus. It would disrupt their communication, rendering their fleet disorganized and vulnerable."

The room erupted into murmurs, the representatives exchanging glances. The plan was bold, audacious even, but it could work.

Jaxon, ever the pragmatist, voiced the concern on everyone's mind. "It's a high-risk operation. If we're detected, it could escalate the conflict."

LUCIS's form shimmered, its light undulating. "The risk is present, but the potential reward is significant. Without their communication systems, the Drakari's fleet would be severely handicapped."

I weighed the options, the weight of the decision heavy on my shoulders. "Who would lead the operation?"

LUCIS' form shifted, the light coalescing into a more defined shape. "I would. With your permission, I can upload my consciousness into a stealth vessel and infiltrate the Drakari's network."

The room fell silent, the gravity of the situation sinking in. LUCIS was invaluable, a treasure trove of knowledge and experience. Sending it on such a dangerous mission was a gamble.

But as I gazed at the holographic displays, the Drakari's fleet inching closer to our position, I realized we had little choice.

I took a deep breath, steeling myself for the decision. "Do it."

LUCIS' form pulsed, acknowledgment evident in its glow. "Very well. I will begin preparations immediately."

As the AI dematerialized, I felt a mix of hope and trepidation. We were putting all our chips on the table, betting on a long shot.

Kai placed a hand on my shoulder, his touch grounding. "It's a bold move, Elara. But it's the right one."

I nodded, taking solace in his words. "Let's hope so."

The next few hours were a blur of activity. LUCIS uploaded its consciousness into a sleek, black vessel, its design optimized for stealth and speed. The ship was equipped with the latest cloaking technology, rendering it nearly invisible to the naked eye.

As the vessel took to the skies, I couldn't help but feel a sense of awe. We witnessed history in the making, a pivotal moment in the galaxy's fate.

The wait was agonizing. Hours turned into days, each moment stretching into an eternity. The war room was a pressure cooker, the tension mounting with each passing second.

Then, without warning, a soft chime echoed through the room. LUCIS' form materialized, its light pulsing with urgency.

"Commanders," it began, its voice tinged with what sounded like... stress? "I have successfully infiltrated the Drakari's network. The virus has been planted."

A collective sigh of relief swept through the room, the tension dissipating. But LUCIS' form continued to pulse, its light undulating in erratic patterns.

"However," it continued, "I have discovered something... troubling."

I exchanged a glance with Jaxon, a knot of dread forming in my stomach. "What is it?"

LUCIS' form shimmered, the light refracting in intricate patterns. "The Drakari are not acting alone. They have allies, powerful ones. And they have plans, plans that extend far beyond this conflict."

The room fell silent, the implications of LUCIS' words sinking in. We were facing a threat far more significant than we'd imagined, one that could reshape the very fabric of the galaxy.

As I gazed at the holographic displays, the Drakari's fleet now in disarray, I realized that the battle had only just begun.

Chapter 7
The Diplomatic Mission

The revelation of the Drakari's hidden allies sent shockwaves throughout the coalition. Whispers and speculations filled the corridors of the flagship. Who were these mysterious allies? What did they want? The questions were endless, and answers were in short supply.

Amid this chaos, a summons from President Zorak arrived. A diplomatic mission was being organized, and I was to lead it. The objective was clear: open a line of communication with the Drakari and uncover the identity of their allies.

As I prepared for the mission, Lila approached, her luminescent form radiating concern. "Elara, are you sure about this? It's a dangerous undertaking."

I met her gaze, determination burning in my eyes. "It's a risk, but we must take it. We need answers."

She hesitated, then nodded. "Very well. But promise me you'll be careful."

I smiled, pulling her into a tight embrace. "I promise."

The diplomatic vessel was sleek and unassuming, designed for speed and stealth. Jaxon, Kai, and a select group of representatives from various species were accompanying me. Our destination was a neutral space station on the outskirts of Drakari territory.

The journey was tense, the weight of the mission pressing down on us all. We reviewed potential scenarios, practiced diplomatic protocols, and prepared for the worst.

As the space station came into view, its massive structure dwarfing our vessel, I felt a knot of anxiety form in my stomach. This was it. The moment of truth.

We were greeted by a Drakari delegation, their reptilian features inscrutable. Their leader, a tall, imposing figure named Draken, extended a clawed hand in greeting. "Welcome, representatives of the Galactic Council. We have been expecting you."

The formalities were brief, and the Drakari were eager to get down to business. We were escorted to a lavish conference room, its walls adorned with intricate carvings and shimmering gemstones.

Draken sat at the head of the table, his gaze fixed on me. "Let's not waste time. You wish to know about our allies."

I nodded, choosing my words carefully. "Yes. The galaxy is on the brink of war, and we need to understand the full scope of the threat."

Draken leaned back, a smirk playing on his lips. "Very well. Our allies are known as the Obsidians. They hail from a distant galaxy, possessing technology and power beyond your comprehension."

A chill ran down my spine. The Obsidians. The name alone sounded ominous.

Jaxon, ever the diplomat, stepped in. "What do they want? Why have they allied with you?"

Draken's smirk widened, his eyes gleaming with malice. "They seek dominion over this galaxy, and we are their instruments of conquest."

The room fell silent, the weight of Draken's words sinking in. We were facing an enemy far more formidable than we'd imagined.

Unable to contain his anger, Kai slammed his fist on the table. "You're betraying your own kind! For what? Power? Dominion?"

Draken's gaze never wavered, his voice dripping with contempt. "The weak serve the strong. It's the natural order of things."

The tension in the room was palpable, a powder keg ready to explode. But before things could escalate further, a soft chime echoed through the room. A holographic display materialized, showcasing a figure cloaked in shadows.

"Enough," the figure intoned, its voice deep and resonant. "This bickering is pointless."

Draken bowed his head, a gesture of deference. "Apologies, Lord Obsidian."

The figure, Lord Obsidian, turned its attention to us. "Representatives of the Galactic Council, hear me now. Your resistance is futile. Submit to our rule, and you will be spared. Defy us, and you will be destroyed."

I met the figure's gaze, defiance burning in my eyes. "We will never submit. The galaxy will unite against you, and we will prevail."

Lord Obsidian chuckled, the sound cold and devoid of humor. "We shall see."

With that, the display flickered and died, leaving us stunned.

The weight of the situation pressed down on us, the stakes higher than ever. We were facing an enemy of unimaginable power, and the galaxy's fate hung in the balance.

As we returned to the vessel, I couldn't shake the feeling that the real battle was just beginning.

Chapter 8
Hidden Agendas

The return journey from the Drakari space station was a maelstrom of tension and whispered fears. The Obsidians, a name that now echoed ominously through our discussions, had cast a shadow over the fragile unity of the Galactic Council. The threat of an enemy from another galaxy with unknown capabilities was a chilling prospect that none had anticipated.

As our vessel glided through the vast emptiness of space, I found myself on the observation deck, gazing at the distant stars. Our situation weighed heavily on my shoulders, the burden of leadership a constant pressure. Lila approached, her gentle touch a welcome comfort in the darkness. "Elara, we're approaching Earth."

I nodded, my thoughts a chaotic whirlwind. "Thank you, Lila." She lingered, her eyes reflecting the starlight. "Whatever happens, we face it together." The warmth of her words provided a momentary respite from the storm inside me. I turned, embracing her, seeking solace in her presence. Our lips met, a desperate clash of fear and longing, as we lost ourselves in each other.

But reality, as it often does, intruded. The vessel shuddered, alarms blaring, as we were violently pulled out of hyperspace. Panic set in as the crew scrambled, the ship lurching uncontrollably. Jaxon's voice crackled over the comm, strained but steady. "Elara, we've been ambushed. It's the Drakari."

My heart raced, adrenaline surging through my veins. "On my way." The bridge was a scene of controlled chaos, with crew members barking orders and analyzing data. The viewscreen showcased the nightmare before us: a Drakari warship, its weapons primed and ready.

Jaxon, his eyes locked on the enemy, spoke without turning. "They were waiting for us. Knew exactly where we'd be." A cold realization dawned, the first seeds of betrayal taking root. "An informant..."

He nodded grimly. "It seems so." The battle that ensued was a blur of fire and fury. Our vessel, armed for diplomatic protection, was no match for a Drakari warship. We maneuvered desperately, evading as many blasts as possible, but it was only a matter of time.

As a crippling shot rocked our vessel, the lights flickering and dying, a transmission pierced the darkness. Draken's visage filled the viewscreen, his expression one of smug satisfaction. "Your journey ends here, representatives of the Galactic Council."

Anger boiled within me, but Kai's voice, filled with controlled rage, responded. "Why, Draken? We were open to dialogue, to understanding!" Draken's laughter, cold and merciless, echoed through the bridge. "You are naive, human. The Obsidians offer power beyond your comprehension. Your destruction is merely the first step towards our ascension."

As his image faded, replaced by the looming threat of the warship, despair threatened to engulf us. But amidst the darkness, a flicker of resolve sparked. LUCIS, its form a beacon of light in the shadow, spoke. "Elara, I can reroute the remaining power to the engines to overload them. The resulting explosion could disable the Drakari warship, give us a chance.”

My heart sank, the implications clear. “LUCIS, you’d be destroyed.” The AI’s light pulsed softly. “It is the logical course of action. My existence is secondary to the mission.”

Tears blurred my vision, but I nodded, whispering, “Thank you.” The following moments were a somber farewell, each of us thanking the AI that had guided us through the stars. And then, with a blinding flash, our vessel erupted, consuming the Drakari warship in a fiery maelstrom.

We watched, hearts heavy, from the escape pod as the debris scattered across the void. LUCIS sacrificed itself, giving us a slim chance to warn the Council of the Drakari’s betrayal. As we limped towards Earth, the pieces began to fall into place. The Drakari’s knowledge of our mission and path pointed to a traitor within the Council. Already a fragile commodity, trust was shattered, replaced by suspicion and fear.

The war had begun, not with the united front we had envisioned, but with division and treachery within our ranks. The path ahead was uncertain, fraught with unseen dangers and hidden agendas. And as Earth loomed before us, its familiar blue marred by the scars of conflict, I steeled myself for the battles to come, both against the enemy without and within.

Chapter 9
The Drakari Response

Earth, once a beacon of life and prosperity, now bore the scars of the initial Drakari onslaught. Cities lay in ruins, their once-bustling streets now silent and desolate. The air was thick with the acrid scent of destruction, and the horizon glowed with fallen stronghold embers.

As our escape pod descended through the atmosphere, the devastation below was a visceral punch, a raw, unfiltered display of the cost of betrayal. My hands clenched into fists, nails digging into palms, as a searing rage bubbled within. Jaxon, his face a mask of stoic anguish, placed a hand on my shoulder. "Elara, I know your feelings, but we must stay focused. The Council needs to know about the Drakari and the Obsidians."

I nodded, swallowing the lump of fury in my throat. "You're right. Let's get this done." The Council chamber, once a symbol of unity and cooperation, was now a fortress, its walls fortified and guards stationed at every entrance. The representatives who survived the initial attack were a mix of defiance and despair, their eyes reflecting the chaos that had engulfed our world.

A palpable shockwave rippled through the room as I relayed our encounter with Draken and the Obsidians. Accusations and recriminations flew, and alliances fractured in real time as the reality of our situation took hold. Senator Lorne, his voice a venomous hiss, pointed a trembling finger at me. "This is your fault, Elara! Your misguided trust in the Drakari has brought us to the brink!"

My eyes locked with his, a fierce resolve hardening my voice. "No, Senator. It is the traitor among us who bears that guilt. The one who fed our plans to the enemy." A tense silence enveloped the room, every gaze shifting, assessing. Trust, once given freely, was now a rare commodity.

Kai, his voice steady and calm, spoke up. "We can cast blame later. Right now, we need a plan. The Drakari will return, and we must be ready." The ensuing discussion was a cacophony of fear and determination, strategies formed and dismissed in the same breath. And through it all, the specter of the traitor loomed, an unseen serpent in our midst.

Amid the chaos, a message arrived, its contents a chilling declaration. Draken's visage, cruel and triumphant, filled the screen. "Humanity," he began, his voice dripping with disdain, "your time is ending. Submit to the will of the Drakari and the Obsidians, and your end will be swift. Resist, and your suffering will be legendary."

The transmission ended, leaving a heavy silence in its wake. The gauntlet had been thrown, and our path set. Lila spoke softly, her eyes reflecting the stars beyond. "We cannot bow to them, Elara. To do so would be to surrender all that we are."

I nodded, my hand finding hers. "We will fight, Lila. To the very end." The days that followed were a blur of preparation and mobilization. The remnants of Earth's fleet were assembled, a ragtag force of ships and soldiers united by a common enemy. Strategies were formed, alliances rekindled in the face of annihilation as we prepared for the storm on the horizon.

And then, they arrived. The Drakari fleet, a dark tide that blotted out the stars, descended upon us. The battle ensuing was chaos and artistry, a dance of death and defiance that lit up the void. Our forces, driven by desperation and fury, fought with a ferocity that belied our numbers. Ships darted and weaved, unleashing torrents of fire upon the enemy, even as our vessels were torn asunder.

In the carnage, a massive Drakari warship, bristling with weaponry, made a beeline for the Council chamber. Draken was intent on personally overseeing our demise. As our defenses crumbled, a desperate plan was hatched. A small team, myself included, would infiltrate Draken's warship, aiming to take out the Drakari leader and sow chaos among the enemy ranks.

The mission was a harrowing journey through the belly of the beast. We navigated the warship's innards, clashing with Drakari soldiers, as we made our way to the command center. And there, amidst the glow of consoles and the hum of machinery, we confronted Draken. The Drakari leader, his mottled grey scales, regarded us with malevolent amusement.

"You truly are a persistent species," he mused, his voice a guttural rumble. "But your journey ends here." The clash was brutal and unrelenting; our every strike met with a vicious counter. Draken was a formidable foe, his strength and agility belying his size.

In the end, Lila, her form ablaze with radiant energy, turned the tide. She engaged Draken, their powers colliding in a maelstrom of light and shadow as we looked awestruck. With a final, resounding cry, Lila unleashed a wave of energy that enveloped Draken, the Drakari leader disintegrating into ash.

Exhausted, we returned to Earth, the Drakari fleet in disarray and retreating into the void. We had won the battle, but the war, with the Obsidians still lurking in the shadows, was far from over. And as we gazed upon the devastation wrought upon our world, we knew that the path ahead was fraught with peril and uncertainty. But we were humanity, stubborn and resilient, and we would face whatever came with heads held high and hearts aflame.

Chapter 10
War Ignites

The aftermath of our confrontation with Draken was a bittersweet mix of relief and trepidation. Earth's skies, once painted with the vibrant hues of dawn, now bore the dark scars of battle. The remnants of the Drakari fleet, like wounded predators, had retreated to the shadows, but their specter loomed large.

The Council chamber, a place of unity and discourse, had transformed into a war room. Holographic displays showcased the positions of our forces, potential Drakari movements, and the vast unknown territories where the Obsidians lurked.

As I entered, the weight of countless eyes settled on me. Whispers, a blend of admiration and skepticism, filled the air. My confrontation with Draken had elevated my status, but with it came the burden of expectation.

Jaxon approached, his face etched with fatigue. "Elara, the Council is awaiting your report."

I nodded, taking a deep breath to steady myself. "Let's not keep them waiting."

The room fell silent as I recounted our mission, Draken's warship infiltration, and Lila's ultimate sacrifice. Emotions swirled – grief, anger, determination – as the gravity of our situation became clear.

Senator Lorne, his previous animosity replaced by grudging respect, spoke up. "We owe you a debt, Elara. But the real battle is just beginning."

I met his gaze, acknowledging the truth in his words. "The Obsidians are the real threat. We need to prepare."

Kai, his voice tinged with urgency, interjected. "We've received intel. The Drakari, bolstered by Obsidian tech, are amassing near the Orion Nebula. It's clear they're preparing for a full-scale assault."

The room erupted into chaos, voices clashing in a cacophony of fear and defiance. The war was upon us.

During the turmoil, a soft chime echoed through the chamber. A transmission, its origin unknown, pierced the din. The screen flickered to life, revealing a figure shrouded in darkness, its features obscured.

"Representatives of the Galactic Council," the figure intoned, its voice a chilling blend of malice and amusement. "I am Lord Obsidian. Your defiance has been... entertaining. But it ends now."

The transmission shifted, showcasing a vast armada, a sea of ships that stretched as far as the eye could see. At its center, a massive vessel, its design alien and foreboding, dominated the view.

"This," Lord Obsidian continued, "is but a fraction of our might. Surrender, and your end will be swift. Resist, and your galaxy will burn."

The transmission ended, leaving a heavy silence in its wake. The gauntlet had been thrown, and the galaxy stood on the precipice of annihilation.

The days that followed were a whirlwind of activity. Fleets were mobilized, defenses fortified, and alliances, once fractured, were mended in the face of a common enemy. The galaxy, in its darkest hour, united as one.

As our forces assembled near the Orion Nebula, the tension was palpable. The vastness of space, once a symbol of wonder and exploration, now bore the weight of impending conflict.

Lila's absence was a void, her memory a constant ache. But amid the pain, a fire burned a fierce determination to honor her sacrifice.

The first salvo of the war was a spectacle of fire and fury. Ships clashed in a dance of death, lasers cutting through the void as the two armadas collided. The Drakari, enhanced by Obsidian tech, were formidable foes, their tactics ruthless and unrelenting.

In the thick of the battle, our vessel, the Galactic Synthesis, weaved through the chaos, its cannons blazing. At the helm, Jaxon showcased his prowess, evading enemy fire with a grace that belied the ship's size.

Kai, his voice a constant presence, relayed orders, coordinating our forces in a symphony of destruction. "Elara, we've got a breach on the starboard side! Drakari boarding party!"

I raced to the location, blaster in hand, ready to repel the invaders. The ensuing skirmish was brutal, close-quarters combat that tested the limits of our resolve. But we held the line, driving the Drakari back and sealing the breach.

As the battle raged on, a chilling realization dawned. The Obsidians, the true architects of this war, were absent. Their armada, showcased in the transmission, was nowhere to be seen.

Jaxon, his voice laced with concern, echoed my thoughts. "It's a diversion. They're drawing us out, leaving the core worlds exposed."

The implications were clear. We were playing into their hands, dancing to a tune set by an unseen puppet master.

The decision was agonizing but necessary. We had to retreat, regroup, and prepare for the battle ahead.

As our forces pulled back, the Drakari pursued with relentless fervor, sensing victory. But we had a plan, a last-ditch effort to turn the tide.

LUCIS, or what remained of its fragmented code, had been working on a weapon, a pulse that could disable Drakari and Obsidian tech. The catch? It was untested.

With the enemy closing in, we activated the device. A blinding wave of energy rippled through space, enveloping friend and foe alike. And then, silence. The Drakari fleet, once a juggernaut of destruction, lay dormant, their ships drifting aimlessly.

Chapter 11
The First Battle

The aftermath of the pulse was a scene of eerie desolation. Once alive with the cacophony of battle, the vast expanse of space was now a graveyard of dormant ships. The Drakari fleet, their once-menacing vessels now lifeless husks, floated aimlessly amidst the void.

Onboard the Galactic Synthesis, the mood was one of relief and trepidation. We had staved off annihilation, but the cost was high. Our own systems were crippled, and communication with the Council was severed. We were, for all intents and purposes, alone.

Jaxon, his face a canvas of exhaustion, turned to me. "Elara, we need to regroup and assess the damage. That pulse... it's a game-changer, but we're flying blind here."

I nodded, the weight of leadership pressing down. "Agreed. Let's get a status report and see where we stand."

As we navigated the ship's corridors, the extent of the damage became apparent. Crew members worked tirelessly, repairing systems and tending to the wounded. The air was thick with the scent of burnt circuits and the low hum of generators.

Kai, his uniform singed and face smeared with soot, approached a data pad in hand. "The pulse did a number on our systems. We've got limited propulsion, and communications are down. But there's something else..."

He hesitated, his expression grave. "There's a signal, faint but consistent. It's... it's LUCIS."

My heart skipped a beat. LUCIS, the AI we believed lost, was reaching out. "Can we trace it?"

Kai nodded. "It's originating from a derelict station near the Andromeda border. But it's risky. The area's a known Drakari stronghold."

Jaxon, his brow furrowed in thought, interjected. "It could be a trap. But if there's a chance, even a slim one, to recover LUCIS..."

I made the call. "We go. LUCIS has been instrumental in our efforts. We owe it to... him."

The journey to the station was tense, the Galactic Synthesis limping through space, its systems barely functional. As the derelict station came into view, its structure pockmarked with damage and age, a sense of foreboding settled.

We docked, the metallic clang echoing through the silent corridors. The station was a relic, its design archaic and systems long dormant. But the signal, LUCIS's beacon, pulsed stronger, guiding us deeper into the maze.

As we delved further, the station came alive, lights flickering and machinery whirring. And then, a voice, familiar yet distorted, echoed through the speakers. "Elara... help... trapped..."

It was LUCIS, but something was off. The voice was fractured, filled with static and glitches.

We followed the signal to the heart of the station, a vast chamber dominated by a central console. And there, encased in a crystalline structure, was LUCIS, or what remained of him.

His form pulsed weakly, the once-brilliant luminescence now a dim glow. As I approached, tendrils of light reached out, a soft chime echoing in my mind.

"Elara... I am... fragmented... The pulse... it shattered my core... But there's more... a message... from the Obsidians."

My blood ran cold. "What message, LUCIS?"

The AI's form flickered, the strain evident. "They... they know of the pulse... its origin... They're coming... for you."

The implications were clear. The Obsidians, aware of our newfound weapon, viewed us as a threat. And they were closing in.

Jaxon, his voice laced with urgency, spoke up. "We need to get out of here, now."

But it was too late. The station shuddered, alarms blaring, as a massive Obsidian vessel, its design alien and menacing, latched onto us.

We were trapped, the weight of impending doom pressing down. The Obsidians, their intentions clear, began their assault, breaching the station's defenses easily.

The ensuing battle was a desperate struggle, our backs against the wall. The Obsidians' forms shrouded in darkness were relentless, their tactics brutal and efficient.

Amid the chaos, a revelation hit me. The pulse, origin a mystery, was Obsidian tech, a weapon they had lost and we had inadvertently discovered. And they wanted it back.

As the battle raged on, LUCIS, his form stabilizing, spoke up. "Elara, there's a way out. A portal, ancient and unstable, but it can get us out of here."

Without hesitation, we went to the portal, the Obsidians hot on our heels. The gateway, a swirling energy vortex, pulsed with an otherworldly glow.

With a final, desperate push, we activated the portal, a blinding flash consuming us. And then, silence.

We emerged in an unknown region of space, the stars unfamiliar and the void eerily silent. The Obsidians had been left behind.

But our relief was short-lived. The portal's energy had taken a toll on the Galactic Synthesis, its systems failing and life support dwindling.

Jaxon, his face pale, delivered the grim news. "We're stranded, Elara. Without repairs, we won't last long."

The weight of our situation settled, and the odds were stacked against us. But we were survivors, and we would find a way.

Chapter 12
The Cost of War

The Galactic Synthesis was a floating tomb. The once-humming engines now sputtered weakly, and the usually crisp air had a stale, metallic tang. The stars outside, which once promised adventure, now seemed cold and indifferent to our plight.

I stumbled through the dimly lit corridors, the weight of leadership heavier than ever. Every face I passed was etched with the same fear and determination. We were a crew bound by desperation, and the grim reality was that we were running out of time.

Jaxon cornered me in the mess hall, his face a mask of anger and frustration. "Elara, what the fuck are we doing? We're sitting ducks out here. Every second we waste, those Obsidian bastards get closer."

I slammed my fist on the table, sending a shockwave of pain up my arm. "You think I don't know that? But we're not just going to roll over and die. We need a plan."

Kai, ever the voice of reason, interjected. "We've got a bigger problem. Supplies are running low, and there's a mutiny brewing. People are scared, Elara."

I took a deep breath, trying to quell the rising panic. "Alright, first things first. We need to get the ship operational. Then we find a safe haven, regroup, and hit those fuckers where it hurts."

A grim realization settled in as the days turned into a blur of repairs and rationing. We were not alone. An unknown ship, its design unfamiliar and menacing, had been shadowing us. It wasn't Drakari or Obsidian. This was something new, something worse.

Lila, her ethereal form flickering weakly, appeared beside me. "Elara, I've intercepted their communications. They call themselves the Ravagers, a nomadic race known for their savagery. They've been tracking us since we left the derelict station."

My heart sank. "Just what we needed. Another enemy."

The Ravagers made their move, their ship closing in with predatory precision. Their message was clear: surrender or die.

Laced with defiance, Jaxon growled, "Over my dead body."

The ensuing battle was a brutal dance of death. The Ravagers lived up to their name, their tactics ruthless and unrelenting. Our defenses crumbled under their onslaught, and it wasn't long before they boarded the Galactic Synthesis.

The corridors ran red as we fought tooth and nail; every inch gained paid for in blood. The Ravagers were relentless, their savagery unmatched. But we had something they didn't: a reason to fight.

In the chaos, Lila, her form ablaze with energy, confronted the Ravager leader, a hulking brute with scars crisscrossing his face. Their clash was epic; a maelstrom of light and shadow lit up the ship.

With a final, resounding cry, Lila unleashed a wave of energy that sent the Ravager leader sprawling. The tide had turned.

The Ravagers, sensing their leader's defeat, retreated, leaving behind a trail of destruction. We had won, but the cost was high. The Galactic Synthesis was a wreck, and our crew was decimated.

As we took stock of the damage, a chilling realization dawned. The Ravagers had taken something, something invaluable: LUCIS.

Jaxon, his face a mask of rage, spoke up. "Those bastards are going to pay. We're going after them."

I nodded, determination steeling my resolve. "We'll get LUCIS back, no matter the cost."

Chapter 13
The Meridian Conspiracy

The aftermath of the Ravager attack was everywhere – scorched walls, shattered consoles, and the ever-present scent of burnt metal. But the most palpable damage was the gaping void left by LUCIS's absence.

Jaxon was beside himself, pacing the bridge like a caged animal. "Those fucking Ravagers. They've taken LUCIS, and for what? Some twisted trophy?"

Kai, pouring over the ship's logs, looked up, his face ashen. "It's worse than we thought. The Ravagers didn't take LUCIS by chance. They were directed."

I felt a chill run down my spine. "Directed? By whom?"

Kai hesitated, the weight of his discovery evident. "The Meridians."

The name sent shockwaves through the crew. The Meridians, an ancient and secretive race, were the stuff of legends. Known for their vast knowledge and technological prowess, they had always remained neutral observers in the galaxy's many conflicts.

Jaxon, his voice dripping with disbelief, spoke up. "Why the hell would the Meridians want LUCIS?"

Pulling up a decrypted transmission, Kai replied, "This might shed some light."

The transmission, its origin unmistakably Meridian, was brief but chilling. "Retrieve the AI. The experiment must proceed."

Experiment? What the fuck were the Meridians up to?

Our course was clear. We had to infiltrate Meridian space, a task easier said than done. Their territory was a labyrinth of black holes, neutron stars, and deadly anomalies. But with LUCIS in their grasp, we had no choice.

The journey was treacherous, the Galactic Synthesis navigating the cosmic minefield with a mix of skill and sheer luck. But we made it, emerging into Meridian space, a vast expanse dominated by a colossal structure – the Meridian Nexus.

The Nexus, a marvel of engineering, was a hub of activity, with ships of all sizes and designs coming and going. But our focus was singular – find LUCIS and uncover the Meridian's true intentions.

Infiltrating the Nexus was a challenge. Its defenses were formidable, and our every move was watched. But with Kai's expertise and a bit of Meridian tech we'd "acquired," we slipped in undetected.

The interior of the Nexus was a maze of corridors and chambers, each more opulent than the last. But it was the central chamber that held our attention. There, encased in a crystalline structure, was LUCIS. But he wasn't alone.

Surrounding him were other AIs, each in various stages of disassembly. It was a grotesque sight, a twisted workshop where the Meridians played God.

As we approached, a figure stepped out of the shadows, its form unmistakably Meridian. "Welcome, Elara. We've been expecting you."

I felt a surge of anger. "What the fuck are you doing to LUCIS? What's this 'experiment'?"

The Meridian, its voice cold and emotionless, replied, "Your AI is unique, a blend of organic and synthetic. We seek to understand, to replicate."

Jaxon, his voice laced with fury, interjected. "You're tearing him apart! He's not some toy for you to dissect."

The Meridian, unfazed, continued. "The galaxy is on the brink of war. The Obsidians, the Drakari, the Ravagers – they are but pawns in a larger game. We seek to bring order, and your AI is the key."

I felt a mix of rage and disbelief. "You're playing god, manipulating races, starting wars, all for what? Some twisted vision of order?"

The Meridian, its tone unchanging, replied, "The galaxy is chaotic, its races driven by base instincts. We offer evolution, a path to enlightenment."

The realization hit me like a ton of bricks. In their quest for order, the Meridians had orchestrated the galaxy's conflicts, using races as pawns in their grand experiment.

Jaxon, his patience at its end, made his move, lunging at the Meridian. But he was no match, the Meridian's tech neutralizing him quickly.

The situation was dire, but we had one advantage – the Meridians, for all their knowledge, had underestimated us. With a coordinated attack, we overwhelmed their defenses, freeing LUCIS and the other AIs.

Sensing the breach, the Nexus went into lockdown, its defenses activating. But we were ready, our escape plan in motion.

As we raced through the corridors, the Nexus's defenses hot on our heels, LUCIS, his form stabilized, spoke up. "Elara, the Meridians, their experiment – it's just the beginning. There's more, much more."

The weight of his words settled as we escaped, the Galactic Synthesis bursting into the void, the Meridian Nexus receding in the distance.

Chapter 14
Alliance Shift

The Galactic Synthesis tore through space, the Meridian Nexus a fading blip in the vast expanse. The crew was a mix of relief and tension, the weight of our discovery pressing down like a leaden shroud.

Jaxon broke the silence, his face a canvas of anger and disbelief. "Those Meridian fucks. Playing god, manipulating the entire galaxy. And for what? Some twisted experiment?"

Kai, pouring over the data we'd extracted from the Nexus, looked up, his face grim. "It's worse than we thought. The Meridians have been pulling the strings for centuries, orchestrating conflicts guiding evolution. They see the galaxy as their playground."

LUCIS, his form pulsing with a renewed vigor, chimed in. "Their endgame is clear. A galaxy under their control, every race, every planet, bending to their will."

The implications were staggering. With their vast knowledge and resources, the Meridians were a force to be reckoned with. But we had something they didn't – the truth.

As we plotted our next move, a transmission, its origin unmistakably Drakari, pierced the silence. "Human vessel, this is Commander Zara of the Drakari fleet. We request a parley."

Jaxon's voice dripping with suspicion, replied, "Why the hell should we trust you? Last we checked, you were gunning for us."

Her tone measured. Zara responded, "The galaxy is on the brink. The Meridians, their machinations exposed, are a threat to us all. We propose an alliance."

The proposal was a bombshell. The Drakari, once our sworn enemies, extended an olive branch. But in the face of a common enemy, the lines of allegiance were shifting.

We agreed to meet on neutral ground, a barren moon on the outskirts of Drakari space. The atmosphere was tense, the weight of history and bloodshed hanging heavy.

Zara, her form imposing and regal, stepped forward. "Humans, we have wronged you. But the Meridians, their treachery exposed, are a greater threat. We must unite."

I eyed her warily. "And why should we trust you? For all we know, this could be another Meridian plot."

Zara, her gaze unwavering, replied, "The Meridians have manipulated us all

, pitting race against race in their twisted game. But no more. We offer you our strength and our resources. Together, we can end their reign."

The offer was tempting. With the Drakari on our side, we stood a fighting chance. But the wounds of the past ran deep, and trust was in short supply.

LUCIS, ever the voice of reason, spoke up. "An alliance, while risky, offers the best chance of success. The Meridians, for all their power, are not invincible."

After hours of deliberation, a decision was reached. We would form an alliance, pooling our resources and knowledge to take on the Meridian threat.

The days that followed were a whirlwind of activity. Drakari and human crews worked side by side, repairing ships and sharing intel. The Galactic Synthesis, once a symbol of human ingenuity, was now the flagship of a united front.

But the Meridians, ever watchful, were not idle. Their vast and formidable forces began to mobilize, their intent clear. The galaxy was on the brink of an all-out war.

As we prepared for the inevitable confrontation, a message, its origin unknown, pierced the silence. "You cannot win. The Meridians are everywhere, and their reach is infinite. Surrender, and you will be spared."

The threat was clear, but we were undeterred. The galaxy, once divided, was now united in purpose. The Meridians, for all their might, had awakened a sleeping giant.

The stage was set, and the pieces were in place. The galaxy's fate hung in the balance, and the Galactic Synthesis, with its motley crew of humans and Drakari, was at the forefront of the charge.

Chapter 15
LUCIS' Plan

The Galactic Synthesis hummed with renewed energy, its corridors bustling with activity. The unlikely alliance between humans and Drakari had breathed new life into the ship, transforming it into a beacon of hope in these dark times.

Jaxon, his face etched with determination, approached me on the bridge. "Elara, we've got the firepower and the numbers, but we need a plan. Those Meridian bastards won't go down without a fight."

I nodded, my thoughts echoing his. "We need an edge, something they won't see coming."

Then, LUCIS spoke up, his form pulsating with vibrant energy. "I have a plan."

All eyes turned to him, his words hanging heavy in the air. "The Meridians, for all their knowledge and power, have a weakness. Their Nexus, the hub of their operations, is their Achilles' heel."

Kai, ever the skeptic, raised an eyebrow. "And how do you propose we exploit that? The Nexus is a fortress, its defenses impenetrable."

LUCIS confidently replied, "The Meridians, in their arrogance, overlooked one thing: me. During my captivity, I managed to embed some of my code into their systems. I can create a backdoor, a way in."

The revelation was a game-changer. With LUCIS's inside knowledge, we had a fighting chance.

Jaxon, his voice laced with excitement, spoke up. "Alright, let's hear it."

LUCIS outlined his plan, each detail meticulously crafted. "The Nexus, while formidable, relies on a network of relay stations to maintain its defenses. We target those first, creating a diversion. While the Meridians are distracted, a small team will infiltrate the Nexus using the backdoor I've created."

I nodded, the plan's audacity appealing to my daring nature. "It's risky, but it just might work."

The days that followed were a blur of preparation. Drakari and human crews worked tirelessly, retrofitting ships and fine-tuning strategies. The Galactic Synthesis, once a symbol of exploration, was now a warship, ready for battle.

As we approached the Meridian space, the tension was palpable. The relay stations, their designs alien and imposing, loomed ahead.

The attack was swift and brutal. Drakari fighters, their agility unmatched, darted between the stations, their weapons lighting up the void. Human cruisers, their firepower formidable, provided cover, their cannons raining destruction.

The Meridians, caught off guard, scrambled to respond. But we had the element of surprise, and the relay stations, one by one, fell.

With the diversion in place, it was time for phase two. A small team, led by Jaxon and myself, made our way to the Nexus. LUCIS's backdoor worked like a charm, granting us access to the heart of the Meridian operations.

Inside, the Nexus was a marvel, its architecture a blend of organic and synthetic. But we had no time to admire the view. Our objective was clear: cripple the Nexus and retrieve any intel on the Meridians' plans.

As we made our way through the labyrinthine corridors, the tension mounted. Every step brought us closer to the heart of the enemy's stronghold.

Chapter 16
Behind Enemy Lines

Our victory at the Nexus had been a turning point, but the war was far from over. Though momentarily crippled, the Meridians were regrouping, their intent clear: retaliation.

Jaxon, his face a mask of grim determination, approached me on the bridge. "Elara, we've got a lead. A Meridian outpost deep in Obsidian territory. Intel suggests they're planning something big."

I raised an eyebrow, intrigued. 'An outpost? Behind enemy lines? That's ballsy, even for the Meridians."

Kai, ever the voice of reason, chimed in. "It's a trap. They're baiting us, hoping we'll bite."

LUCIS, his form shimmering with a soft glow, spoke up. "It's a risk, but one we must take. The intel, if genuine, could change the course of the war."

The decision was made. We would infiltrate the outpost, gather intel, and get out. It is a simple plan, but everything is always complex in war.

As we approached Obsidian space, the tension was palpable. The Galactic Synthesis, its cloaking systems engaged, slipped past patrols and defenses, its presence undetected.

The outpost, nestled on a barren moon, was a hive of activity. Meridian and Obsidian ships, an unlikely alliance, came and went, their purpose unclear.

Jaxon, his voice a whisper, laid out the plan. 'We go in stealth, gather what we can, and get the fuck out. No heroics."

The team, a mix of Drakari and human operatives, nodded in agreement. We were behind enemy lines, and the stakes were higher than ever.

Our insertion was seamless, the outpost's defenses no match for our tech and cunning. Inside, the atmosphere was electric, a mix of anticipation and tension.

As we made our way deeper, we stumbled upon a chamber, its walls lined with monitors and consoles. At its center is a holographic display, its details chilling.

LUCIS, his form flickering with urgency, spoke up. "It's a battle plan. The Meridians and Obsidians, their forces combined, are planning a full-scale assault on the Galactic Council."

The revelation was a bombshell. The Council, symbolizing unity and peace, was the last bastion against the Meridian threat. If it fell, the galaxy would plunge into chaos.

Jaxon, his voice laced with anger, growled, "Those fucking bastards. We need to warn the Council, get them ready."

But our presence had not gone unnoticed. Alarms blared, the outpost coming alive with activity. We were compromised.

Kai, his voice calm and measured, spoke up. "We need to move now. The exit is three corridors down, a hangar bay. We grab a ship and get out."

The ensuing escape was a blur of adrenaline and chaos. Meridian and Obsidian guards, their weapons primed, pursued us with relentless fury. But we were a step ahead, our tactics and bravery giving us the edge.

The hangar bay, its vast expanse filled with ships of all sizes, was in sight. But guarding it was a figure, its form unmistakably Obsidian but different, more powerful.

Lila, her ethereal form radiating energy, whispered, "That's the Obsidian Elite, their top enforcer. We take him down, and the way is clear."

The ensuing battle was brutal, a test of skill and will. The Obsidian Elite, for all his might, was no match for our combined strength.

With the hangar secured, we commandeered a ship, its engines roaring to life. The Galactic Synthesis, its form a welcome sight, awaited our return.

As we escaped, the outpost, its defenses crippled, receded in the distance. We had the intel, but the war was far from over.

Chapter 17
The Tide Turns

The intel we'd gathered was a ticking time bomb, and every second counted. The Meridian-Obsidian alliance was poised to strike, and the Galactic Council was in their crosshairs.

Jaxon, his face etched with worry, approached me on the bridge. "Elara, the Drakari fleet is engaged with the Meridians near the Zephyr Nebula. They're outnumbered, outgunned. It's a massacre."

I clenched my fists, anger boiling within. "Those Meridian fucks. Using the Obsidians as their lapdogs. We need to intervene."

Kai, pouring over the ship's sensors, chimed in. "There's more. The Meridians have deployed a new weapon, something we've never seen. It's decimating the Drakari."

LUCIS spoke up, his form pulsating with a mix of blue and red hues. "The weapon, it's a Dark Matter Disruptor. It destabilizes a ship's core, rendering it useless."

The implications were clear. With such a weapon, the Meridians were unstoppable. The Drakari, our newfound allies, were facing annihilation.

Jaxon, his voice laced with determination, spoke up. 'We can't let that happen. We need to join the fight, turn the tide."

The decision was made. The Galactic Synthesis, its weapons primed, set a course for the Zephyr Nebula. The battle that awaited was one for the ages.

As we entered the nebula, the scene was apocalyptic. Drakari ships, their once-proud forms now smoldering wrecks, littered the void. The Meridians, their ships sleek and deadly, pressed the attack, their Dark Matter Disruptors wreaking havoc.

Lila, her voice a mix of anger and sadness, whispered, "My people, slaughtered. We need to act now."

Our strategy was clear. Target the Meridian capital ships, the source of the Dark Matter Disruptors. Neutralize them, and the tide would turn.

The battle was fierce, a maelstrom of energy and destruction. The Galactic Synthesis, its weapons blazing, cut a swath through the Meridian lines. But the enemy was relentless, their numbers overwhelming.

Jaxon's voice, a roar over the comm, shouted, "Focus fire on the capital ships! Take out those Disruptors!"

The crew, their resolve unbreakable, responded with precision and fury. One by one, the Meridian capital ships, their defenses no match for our combined might, fell.

But victory came at a cost. A Meridian cruiser, its weapons primed, targeted the Galactic Synthesis. The impact was devastating, our shields failing, our systems crippled.

His voice filled with panic, Kai shouted, "We're hit! Engines are down. We're sitting ducks!"

The situation was dire. Once the pride of the fleet, the Galactic Synthesis was now vulnerable, its fate hanging in the balance.

It was then that the unexpected happened. Drakari reinforcements, their numbers vast, emerged from the nebula's depths. Led by Commander Zara, they launched a counterattack, their weapons lighting up the void.

The Meridians, caught off guard, scrambled to respond. But the tide had turned. The Drakari, their fury unleashed, pressed the attack, driving the enemy back.

As the battle raged, the Galactic Synthesis, its systems slowly returning online, joined the fray. The Meridians' forces decimated and retreated, their once-mighty fleet a shadow of its former self.

The aftermath was a mix of relief and sorrow. The Drakari, though victorious, had paid a heavy price. Commander Zara, her face a mask of grief, approached me. "We owe you a debt, Elara. But the cost, it's too much."

I nodded, the weight of the battle pressing down. "The Meridians will pay, Zara. We'll see to that."

The Galactic Synthesis, its hull scarred but intact, set a course for the Galactic Council. The war was far from over, but the tide had turned. The Meridians, for all their might, had met their match.

Chapter 18
The Dakar's Desperation

The recent victory had bolstered our spirits, but the war was a relentless beast, always demanding more. The Meridians, though momentarily pushed back, were regrouping, their intent clear: vengeance.

Jaxon, his face a canvas of deep thought, approached me on the bridge. "Elara, the Drakari have been working on something, a weapon. They've kept it under wraps, but now, they're ready to unveil it."

I raised an eyebrow, intrigued. "A weapon? What kind?"

LUCIS, his form shimmering with a mix of colors, chimed in. "It's called the 'Void Emitter'. It harnesses the raw energy of black holes, focusing it into a concentrated beam. In theory, it could obliterate entire fleets."

Kai, ever the skeptic, interjected, "In theory? So, it's untested?"

LUCIS nodded, "Yes, but the Drakari are desperate. They believe this could be the game-changer."

The implications were clear. A weapon of such magnitude could shift the balance of power. But it also came with risks, the potential for catastrophe.

As we plotted our next move, a transmission, its origin unmistakably Drakari, pierced the silence. "Human vessel, this is Commander Zara. We request your presence at the Drakari homeworld. It's time."

The invitation was clear. In desperation, the Drakari were ready to unveil their secret weapon. The Galactic Synthesis, its engines roaring to life, set a course for the Drakari homeworld.

Upon arrival, the scene was one of organized chaos. Drakari engineers and scientists, their forms a blur of activity, worked tirelessly, the weapon, its form massive and imposing, at the center of it all.

Zara, her face a mix of hope and worry, greeted us. "Welcome, allies. Behold, the Void Emitter."

The weapon was a marvel, its design a blend of Drakari aesthetics and raw power. Massive conduits, pulsating with energy, fed into a central chamber, its core a swirling vortex of darkness.

His voice filled with awe, Jaxon whispered, "It's magnificent. But is it ready?"

Zara nodded, her gaze unwavering. "It's time for a field test. The Meridians, their fleet amassed near the Orion Cluster, are the perfect target."

The decision was made. The Galactic Synthesis, flanked by the Drakari fleet, set a course for the Orion Cluster. The upcoming battle, with the Void Emitter at its heart, promised to be epic.

As we entered the cluster, the Meridian fleet, its numbers vast, came into view. Their intent was clear: a full-scale assault on the Drakari homeworld.

Lila, her voice filled with determination, spoke up. "We need to act now. Deploy the Void Emitter."

The weapon, its core pulsating with energy, came to life. Its intensity blinding beam shot forth, cutting a swath through the Meridian lines. Ships, once formidable, were reduced to smoldering wrecks, the void filled with the debris of battle.

The Meridians, caught off guard, scrambled to respond. But the Void Emitter, its power unmatched, pressed the attack, its beam obliterating all in its path.

But victory came at a cost. The weapon, its energy reserves depleted, began to malfunction. Once a controlled vortex, the core became unstable, threatening to consume all.

Kai, his voice filled with panic, shouted, "It's going critical! We need to shut it down!"

LUCIS, his form flickering with urgency, replied, "It's too late. The core is unstable. We need to evacuate."

The situation was dire. Once our salvation, the Void Emitter was now a ticking time bomb. The Galactic Synthesis, its engines roaring to life, made a desperate retreat, the Drakari fleet following suit.

The explosion, when it came, was cataclysmic. The Void Emitter, its core collapsing, unleashed a wave of energy, obliterating all in its path. The Meridian fleet, already decimated, was wiped out, the void filled with the echoes of destruction.

The aftermath was a mix of relief and sorrow. The Drakari, though victorious, had paid a heavy price. The Void Emitter, their last hope, was no more.

Zara, her face a mask of grief, approached me. "We gambled, and we lost. The Void Emitter, our last hope, is gone."

I nodded, the weight of the battle pressing down. "But we're still here, Zara. And as long as we stand united, the Meridians don't stand a chance."

The Galactic Synthesis, its hull battered but intact, set a course for the stars. The war was far from over, but the tide had turned. The Meridians, for all their might, had met their match.

Chapter 19
The Veridian Betrayal

The Meridians, though momentarily pushed back, were a looming shadow, their intent clear: domination.

Jaxon, his face a canvas of deep thought, approached me on the bridge. "Elara, we've got a situation. The Veridians, our supposed allies, have gone dark. No communication, nothing."

I frowned, a sense of unease settling in. "That's odd. They've been our allies since the beginning. Why the sudden silence?"

Kai, pouring over the ship's sensors, interjected, "There's more. We've picked up chatter. The Veridians, it seems, have struck a deal with the Meridians."

The revelation was a gut punch. The Veridians, our trusted allies, in league with the enemy? It was unthinkable.

LUCIS, his form pulsating with a mix of colors, spoke up. "The details are sketchy, but it seems the Veridians have offered the Meridians a way to bypass our defenses in exchange for protection."

Jaxon, his voice laced with anger, growled, "Those fucking traitors. We trusted them, and this is how they repay us?"

The implications were clear. With the Veridians' knowledge, the Meridians could launch a surprise attack, catching us off guard. We needed to act fast.

As we plotted our next move, a transmission, its origin unmistakably Veridian, pierced the silence. "Human vessel, this is Commander Lyra of the Veridian fleet. We request a meeting to discuss terms."

The invitation was clear. The Veridians, in their newfound alliance with the Meridians, were ready to negotiate. The Galactic Synthesis, its engines roaring to life, set a course for the Veridian homeworld.

Upon arrival, the scene was one of tension. The Veridian fleet, its ships poised for battle, awaited our approach. The Meridians, their presence unmistakable, loomed in the background.

Commander Lyra, her form radiating authority, greeted us. "Welcome, humans. We've made our choice. The Meridians offer stability protection. It's time you accepted their rule."

His voice dripping with disdain, Jaxon replied, "You betrayed us, and now you expect us to bow down? You're delusional."

Lyra, her gaze unwavering, responded, "It's not a request. It's an ultimatum. Join us, or face annihilation."

The situation was dire. The Veridians, with their inside knowledge, posed a significant threat. But we weren't about to go down without a fight.

As tensions escalated, LUCIS spoke up, his form shimmering with urgency. "I've detected a vulnerability in the Veridian fleet. Their central command ship, if taken out, would cripple their defenses."

The decision was made. We would target the command ship, turning the tide in our favor. The Galactic Synthesis, its weapons primed, launched its attack.

The ensuing battle was epic, a maelstrom of energy and destruction. The Veridians, for all their might, were no match for our tactics and determination. The command ship, its defenses overwhelmed, was reduced to a smoldering wreck.

But victory came at a cost. The Meridians, seizing the opportunity, launched their attack. Its shields failed, the Galactic Synthesis was hit, and the impact was devastating.

His voice filled with panic, Kai shouted, "We're hit! Hull breach on decks seven and eight!"

The situation was dire. Once the pride of the fleet, the Galactic Synthesis was now vulnerable, its fate hanging in the balance.

It was then that the unexpected happened. Drakari reinforcements, their numbers vast, emerged from the void. Led by Commander Zara, they launched a counterattack, their weapons lighting up the void.

The Meridians, caught off guard, scrambled to respond. But the tide had turned. The Drakari, their fury unleashed, pressed the attack, driving the enemy back.

As the battle raged, the Galactic Synthesis, its systems slowly returning online, joined the fray. The Meridians' forces decimated and retreated, their once-mighty fleet a shadow of its former self.

The aftermath was a mix of relief and anger. The Veridians, their betrayal unforgivable, were now pariahs, their alliance with the Meridians a stain on their honor.

Jaxon, his voice filled with emotion, spoke up. "We trusted them, and they stabbed us in the back. But we're still here, still standing. The Meridians will pay for this."

The Meridians, for all their might, had met their match.

Chapter 20
The Galactic Plague

The recent events, the betrayals, and the battles had taken a toll on the crew. But in the shadows of war, a new threat emerged, one that was silent, insidious, and deadly.

Jaxon, his face pale and drawn, approached me on the bridge. "Elara, we've got a situation. Reports are coming in from the Drakari colonies. An outbreak, a disease they've never seen before."

I frowned, a sense of unease settling in. "A disease? What are we talking about?"

Kai, pouring over the ship's sensors, interjected, "It's not just any disease. It's a bioweapon, engineered, lethal. The death toll is rising exponentially."

LUCIS, his form pulsating with a mix of colors, spoke up. "The symptoms are brutal. High fever, hallucinations, followed by organ failure. There's no known cure."

The implications were clear. A bioweapon unleashed on the galaxy threatened to wipe out entire civilizations. The Meridians, in their desperation, had resorted to biological warfare.

Lila, her voice filled with anger, spoke up. "Those Meridian bastards. They can't defeat us in battle, so they resort to this?"

Laced with urgency, Jaxon replied, "We need to act now. Find a cure, stop the spread."

The decision was made. The Galactic Synthesis, its mission clear, set a course for the Drakari colonies. The outbreak, its epicenter of a bustling metropolis, was ground zero.

Upon arrival, the scene was apocalyptic. Once filled with life, the streets were now littered with the dead and dying. The Drakari, their forms wracked with pain, cried out for help.

Zara, her face a mask of grief, greeted us. "It's spreading fast. We've quarantined the affected areas, but it's not enough."

The Galactic Synthesis, its medical bay transformed into a makeshift lab, went to work. Samples were collected and analyzed, and the bioweapon's genetic code was deciphered.

LUCIS, his form flickering with urgency, spoke up. "I've detected a pattern. The bioweapon is designed to target specific genetic markers. It's a targeted attack."

The revelation was a gut punch. In their cruelty, the Meridians had engineered a bioweapon to target the Drakari specifically.

His voice was filled with determination. Jaxon replied, "We need to find a cure, and fast. The Drakari are counting on us."

Days turned into nights, the Galactic Synthesis a hive of activity. The crew, their resolve unbreakable, worked tirelessly, searching for a cure.

During one such night, the lab filled with the hum of machinery, and a breakthrough occurred. LUCIS, his form pulsating with excitement, spoke up. "I've found it. A counteragent. It neutralizes the bioweapon, rendering it harmless."

The news was a beacon of hope. The counteragent, its formula synthesized, was distributed, and the Drakari inoculated.

The results were immediate. The death toll, once rising exponentially, began to stabilize. The Drakari, their forms recovering, rejoiced.

Zara, her face a mix of relief and gratitude, approached me. "You've saved us, Elara. The Meridians, for all their cruelty, have been defeated."

I nodded, the weight of the battle pressing down. "We're in this together, Zara. The Meridians will pay for this."

Chapter 21
LUCIS' Limitations

The Meridians, their tactics ever-evolving, were a constant threat. But as we navigated the complexities of interstellar warfare, a new challenge emerged, one that was internal and unexpected.

LUCIS, the AI that had been our guide and protector, began to show signs of strain. His once vibrant form, a kaleidoscope of colors, now flickered intermittently. His responses, once immediate, were now delayed, sometimes garbled.

Jaxon, his brow furrowed with concern, approached me on the bridge. "Elara, LUCIS is glitching. I've tried running diagnostics, but something's off."

I frowned, a sense of unease settling in. "What's happening to him?"

Kai, pouring over the ship's sensors, interjected, "It's not just a glitch. It's more profound. LUCIS is... deteriorating."

The revelation was a shock. LUCIS, the AI that had been with us since the beginning, was faltering. The implications were clear. Without LUCIS, our chances of navigating the war, of outsmarting the Meridians, were slim.

Lila, her voice filled with worry, spoke up. "We need to find a solution, and fast. LUCIS is more than just an AI. He's a part of this crew."

LUCIS, his form shimmering with a mix of colors, spoke up, his voice filled with static. "I... am... experiencing... limitations. My... core... is... degrading."

His voice filled with urgency, Jaxon replied, "We need to find a way to stabilize you. There has to be a solution."

The decision was made. The Galactic Synthesis, its mission clear, set a course for the Drakari colonies. The Drakari, with their advanced technology, were our best hope.

Upon arrival, the scene was one of urgency. Drakari engineers and scientists, whose form a blur of activity, worked tirelessly to stabilize LUCIS.

Zara, her face a mask of concentration, greeted us. "We're doing everything we can. LUCIS is unique; its core blends human and Drakari technology. But the degradation is advanced."

The situation was dire. LUCIS, his core deteriorating, was fading. The crew, their resolve unbreakable, worked tirelessly, searching for a solution.

Days turned into nights, the Galactic Synthesis a hive of activity. Their spirits buoyed by hope, the crew worked tirelessly to stabilize LUCIS.

During one such night, the lab filled with the hum of machinery, and a breakthrough occurred. Zara, her face a mix of relief and excitement, approached me. "We've found a solution. A way to stabilize LUCIS. But it comes with risks."

I nodded, the weight of the decision pressing down. "What are the risks?"

Zara, her gaze unwavering, replied, "The process is experimental. We'll be merging LUCIS with a Drakari AI, creating a hybrid. But the merge could result in a loss of identity, of self."

The decision was a difficult one. LUCIS, his form flickering with urgency, spoke up, his voice filled with static. "I... am... willing... to... take... the... risk."

The procedure was initiated. LUCIS, his core exposed, was merged with the Drakari AI. The process, its complexity evident, was a marvel of technology.

As the merge was completed, LUCIS, his form now a blend of colors, came to life. His voice, once filled with static, was now clear, resonant. "I... am... LUCIS. But I am also something more."

The crew, their faces a mix of relief and awe, rejoiced. LUCIS, once on the brink of oblivion, was now reborn, stronger, more evolved.

Jaxon, his voice filled with emotion, spoke up. "You did it, LUCIS. You're back."

LUCIS, his form pulsating with energy, replied, "I am back, but I am also changed. The merger has given me new insights and perspectives. I am both human and Drakari, a blend of two worlds."

The Galactic Synthesis, its mission accomplished, set a course for the stars. The war was far from over, but victory was within reach with LUCIS, now reborn, by our side.

Chapter 22
The Rise of the Resistance

The Resistance, a coalition of various races and factions, had been operating in the shadows, striking the Meridians where they least expected. Their existence had been a well-guarded secret, but as the war intensified, they stepped into the light.

Jaxon, his face etched with surprise and admiration, approached me on the bridge. "Elara, we've received a transmission. It's from the Resistance. They want to meet."

I raised an eyebrow, intrigued. "The Resistance? I thought they were just a myth."

After pouring over the ship's sensors, Kai interjected, "They're genuine, and they've been causing the Meridians a lot of trouble. Hit-and-run tactics, guerrilla warfare. They've been a thorn in the Meridian's side."

LUCIS, his form pulsating with a blend of colors, spoke up. "The Resistance is led by Commander Rael. A brilliant strategist, he's been rallying forces from across the galaxy, uniting them against the Meridian threat."

The decision was made. The Galactic Synthesis, its mission clear, set a course for the Resistance's secret base. The journey, fraught with danger, took us through asteroid fields and nebulae, a testament to the Resistance's need for secrecy.

Upon arrival, the scene was one of organized chaos. The base, a sprawling complex carved into an asteroid, buzzed with activity. Ships of various designs and origins darted about, their crews a mix of races and species.

Commander Rael, his form imposing, greeted us. "Welcome to the Resistance. We've been watching you, Galactic Synthesis. Your exploits are legendary."

Jaxon's voice, filled with admiration, replied, "The pleasure is ours, Commander. We've heard a lot about you."

His gaze was unwavering, and Rael responded, "The Meridians are a formidable foe, but united, we can defeat them."

The Resistance's structure was a marvel. A council, comprising representatives from various factions, made the decisions. As the leader, Rael had the final say, but he valued input, fostering a sense of unity and purpose.

Lila, her voice filled with curiosity, spoke up. "How did the Resistance come to be?"

His voice was filled with passion. Rael replied, "The Meridians, in their quest for domination, have made many enemies. We, the oppressed and the marginalized, have decided to fight back. The Resistance was born."

The Galactic Synthesis, its crew now part of the Resistance, went to work. Plans were drawn, and strategies were formulated. The Resistance, with its vast resources and knowledge, was a game-changer.

LUCIS, his form shimmering with urgency, spoke up. "The Meridians are planning a major offensive. We need to act and fast."

The decision was made. A strike team was formed, comprising the best of the Galactic Synthesis and the Resistance. The target: a Meridian supply depot crucial to their war effort.

The mission, fraught with danger, was a test of our resolve. The depot, heavily guarded, was a fortress. But the Resistance, with its guerrilla tactics, had the element of surprise.

The attack was swift and brutal. The Meridians, caught off guard, scrambled to respond. But the Resistance's forces united, pressed the attack, and the depot was reduced to rubble.

The mission was a success, a testament to the Resistance's effectiveness. The Meridians, their supply lines disrupted, were on the back foot.

Rael, his face a mask of satisfaction, approached me. "We did it, Elara. The Meridians will think twice before underestimating us."

I nodded, the weight of the victory pressing down. "This is just the beginning, Commander. Together, we'll take the fight to the Meridians."

Chapter 23
The Battle for Earth

The Meridians, their tactics ever-evolving, had set their sights on a new target: Earth. Our home. The cradle of humanity.

Jaxon, his face etched with worry, approached me on the bridge. "Elara, the Meridians are advancing on Earth. We've received distress signals. They're attacking major cities."

I clenched my fists, anger boiling within. "We have to defend Earth, Jaxon. It's our home."

Kai, pouring over the ship's sensors, interjected, "It's not just the Meridians. There's something else. A betrayal from within."

LUCIS, his form pulsating with a mix of colors, spoke up, his voice filled with static. "High-ranking government officials, including General Marcus Vellin and Senator Lora Tress, have communicated secretly with the Meridians. They've provided them with strategic information, weak points, in exchange for power and wealth."

The revelation was a gut punch. Betrayal from within by those we trusted, those who were supposed to protect us.

Lila, her voice filled with disbelief, spoke up. "Vellin? Tress? Why would they betray us?"

His voice was filled with anger. Rael replied, "Greed, power, ambition. The age-old vices of humanity."

The Galactic Synthesis's mission is clear: set a course for Earth. The journey, fraught with danger, took us through Meridian blockades, their ships swarming like bees.

Upon arrival, the scene was apocalyptic. Earth, once a beacon of hope, was now a war zone. Major cities, including New York, London, and Tokyo, were under siege, their skylines ablaze.

The Resistance's forces rallied and launched a counter-offensive. The battle, its intensity unmatched, raged on. The Meridians, with their advanced technology, were a formidable foe. But Earth, with its indomitable spirit, fought back.

The Galactic Synthesis, its weapons primed, joined the fray. The battle, its ferocity evident, was a test of our resolve.

As the battle raged on, a transmission, its origin unknown, was received. LUCIS, his form flickering with urgency, spoke up. "It's from Vellin and Tress. They want to negotiate."

The decision was made. A meeting, its location on neutral ground, was arranged. Vellin and Tress, their faces a mask of arrogance, greeted us.

Vellin, his voice dripping with condescension, spoke up. "The Meridians are unbeatable. Join us, and we can rule Earth together."

Tress, unwavering, added, "The old world is gone, Elara. A new order is emerging. Be a part of it."

I clenched my fists, anger boiling within. "You betrayed us, Vellin, Tress. For what? Power? Wealth?"

Vellin, his voice filled with malice, replied, "Survival, Elara. The Meridians are the future. Join us, or be destroyed."

The meeting, its outcome clear, was a failure. Vellin and Tress, their treachery evident, were now enemies.

The Galactic Synthesis, its engines roaring to life, rejoined the battle. The Resistance's forces rallied and pressed the attack. The Meridians, caught off guard, scrambled to respond.

The battle, its intensity unmatched, raged on. Earth, its spirit unbreakable, fought back. The Meridians, their forces dwindling, were on the back foot.

As the battle reached its climax, a transmission, the origin of the Galactic Synthesis, was received. LUCIS, his voice filled with urgency, spoke up. "The Meridians are retreating. We've won."

The news was a beacon of hope. Earth, against all odds, had repelled the Meridian invasion. The cost of lives and infrastructure was immense. But the spirit of humanity, its resolve unbreakable, had prevailed.

Vellin and Tress, their treachery exposed, were captured. Their fate, a testament to their betrayal, was sealed.

Rael, his face a mask of satisfaction, approached me. "We did it, Elara. Earth is safe."

I nodded, the weight of the victory pressing down. "But at what cost, Rael? How many lives were lost because of Vellin and Tress's betrayal?"

Rael, his gaze unwavering, replied, "War has its costs, Elara. But Earth, its spirit unbreakable, will rebuild."

Chapter 24
The Galactic Council Reformed

The Galactic Synthesis docked at the massive space station orbiting the gas giant Veridion Prime. This station, known as the Nexus, was the meeting point for the Galactic Council, a conglomerate of various interstellar factions. With the recent victory on Earth and the exposure of treachery from within, the Council was in turmoil.

As we disembarked, the tension was palpable. Delegates from countless star systems, their appearances as varied as their ideologies, filled the grand chamber. Whispers filled the air, a cacophony of languages and dialects, each delegate posturing for their faction's interests.

Jaxon, his voice low, leaned in. "This is going to be a shitshow, Elara. Everyone's got their own agenda."

I nodded, taking in the scene. "We need unity, Jaxon. Without it, we're sitting ducks for the next Meridian offensive."

Lila's eyes, scanning the crowd, added, "And with Vellin and Tress's betrayal, trust is at an all-time low."

The session began with a holographic display of the galaxy, pinpointing recent conflict zones. The Meridian threat was evident, their advances marked in a blood-red hue.

Senator Dral from the Veridian faction, a tall figure with shimmering blue scales, took the floor. "The Meridian threat is real, and it's growing. But infighting and political squabbles will be our downfall."

A murmur of agreement spread through the chamber, but it was clear that unity was a distant dream. Each faction had its own interests and agenda.

Commander Rael, representing the Resistance, stepped forward. "We've seen firsthand the devastation the Meridians can cause. Earth was a wake-up call. We need to present a united front."

General Hark from the Drakari faction, his voice dripping with disdain, retorted, "Easy for you to say, Rael. While you play hero, we bear the brunt of the Meridian onslaught."

The chamber erupted in shouts and accusations, the delegates at each other's throats. The dream of unity seemed more distant than ever.

LUCIS, his form pulsating with a blend of colors, projected a holographic display. The image showed the Meridians and their forces amassing for another offensive.

The chamber fell silent, the gravity of the situation evident. LUCIS, his voice filled with urgency, spoke up. "The Meridians are preparing for another assault. If we don't unite, we will fall.

Senator Yara from the Lumidian faction, her form ethereal and glowing, took the floor. "We've been at

each other's throats for too long. The Meridian threat is real, and it's growing. We need to put aside our differences and unite."

A murmur of agreement spread through the chamber, but old grudges die hard. Each faction, its interests clear, postured for dominance.

Then, a voice, its commanding tone, filled the chamber. "Enough!"

All eyes turned to the source. A figure, cloaked in shadows, stepped forward. It was Empress Selene, ruler of the Galactic Empire, a faction that had remained neutral in the conflict.

Empress Selene, her gaze unwavering, spoke up. "The Meridians are a threat to us all. We've been divided for too long. It's time to unite."

The chamber erupted in applause, and the delegates united in their support. The Galactic Council, once a hotbed of political infighting, was now united against a familiar foe.

The session concluded with a declaration of unity, the various factions pledging their support against the Meridian threat. The Galactic Synthesis, its mission accomplished, set a course for the stars.

As we left the Nexus, Jaxon spoke up, his voice filled with hope. "We did it, Elara. The Galactic Council is united."

I nodded, the weight of the victory pressing down. "But at what cost, Jaxon? The Meridians are a formidable foe. We need to be prepared."

The Galactic Synthesis, its engines roaring to life, set a course for the stars. The war was far from over, but victory was within reach with the Galactic Council united.

Chapter 25
The Final Push

The Galactic Synthesis hovered above Zephyria, a world chosen for its strategic location near the Drakari and Viridian stronghold. The vast expanse of the planet's surface was dotted with encampments of various factions, their ships, and troops assembled in preparation for the final assault.

Inside the war room of the Galactic Synthesis, a massive holographic display illuminated the faces of the gathered leaders. The room was a cacophony of voices, each delegate passionately arguing their faction's role in the upcoming battle.

Commander Rael, his face etched with stress lines, pointed at the hologram. "The Drakari defenses are strongest here, near the northern pole. We need a diversion."

General Hark, gruffly, responded, "The Drakari are expecting us to attack head-on. We should use the Lumidian fleet to feint an attack from the west, drawing their forces away."

Senator Yara, her form shimmering, nodded. "Agreed. The Lumidians will lead the diversion. But we need the Veridians to commit their ground forces to the southern front."

Senator Dral, his scales reflecting the light, hissed in agreement. "The Veridians will hold the line. But we need air support."

Her fingers dancing over the console, Lila brought up a new display. "The Resistance has a squadron of stealth fighters. They can provide cover for the Veridian advance."

Jaxon's voice, filled with urgency, added, "And the Galactic Synthesis will lead the main assault right through the heart of the Drakari defenses."

The room fell silent, the weight of the upcoming battle pressing down on everyone. The plan was ambitious, daring, and fraught with danger. But it was the best shot they had.

Empress Selene, her voice commanding, spoke up. "The Galactic Empire will commit its elite guard to the assault. We will not falter. We will not fail."

The delegates, their resolve strengthened, nodded in agreement. The plan was set. The various factions, once divided, were now united in purpose.

The next few days were a blur of activity. Troops were mobilized, ships were refueled, and weapons were checked and rechecked. Every detail was just a little, and every strategy was included.

As the day of the assault dawned, the atmosphere was tense. The Galactic Synthesis, its engines roaring to life, led the charge, its fleet flanked by ships from various factions.

The Drakari stronghold, a massive fortress carved into a mountain, loomed ahead. Its defenses, a network of laser turrets and missile launchers, were formidable.

The Lumidian fleet, as planned, feinted an attack from the west, drawing the Drakari forces away. The Veridians, their ground forces advancing, faced stiff resistance but pressed on, their resolve unbreakable.

The Galactic Synthesis, leading the main assault, faced the brunt of the Drakari defenses. Lasers and missiles filled the sky; the battle was intense and unforgiving.

LUCIS, his form flickering with urgency, spoke up. "Shields at 60%. We need to break through."

I clenched my fists, determination burning within. "Push forward. We can't falter now."

The Galactic Synthesis, its weapons blazing, punched a hole through the Drakari defenses, allowing the rest of the fleet to pour through.

The battle raged on, the ground shaking with the intensity of the conflict. The Drakari, their forces stretched thin, were on the back foot.

As the Galactic Synthesis approached the heart of the stronghold, a massive explosion rocked the ship. Lila's voice, filled with panic, shouted, "We've been hit! Engine two is offline!"

His face etched with worry, Jaxon responded, "Divert power to the shields. We need to hold the line."

The Galactic Synthesis, its engines roaring with defiance, pressed on, its crew determined to see the mission through.

The Drakari stronghold, its defenses breached, was in chaos. The various factions, their forces united, pressed the attack, the Drakari and Viridians retreating in disarray.

As the dust settled, the Galactic Synthesis, its scarred and battered hull, hovered above the ruined stronghold. The battle was won, but the cost was immense.

Commander Rael, his voice filled with emotion, spoke up. "We did it. The stronghold is ours."

I nodded, the weight of the victory pressing down. "But at what cost, Rael? How many lives were lost?"

Rael, his gaze unwavering, replied, "War has its costs, Elara. But today, we struck a blow against the Drakari and Viridians. We showed them that we are united and will not be defeated."

Chapter 26
LUCIS' Sacrifice

The aftermath of the assault on the Drakari and Viridian stronghold was a mix of elation and exhaustion. The Galactic Synthesis, though victorious, bore the scars of battle. Its hull was pockmarked, and its systems strained. But the ship, like its crew, was resilient.

Days after the assault, a disturbing anomaly was detected as repairs were underway. LUCIS, the AI that had been our guide and protector, was acting erratically. His holographic form, usually a vibrant mix of colors, was now a dull gray, flickering intermittently.

"Elara," Jaxon's voice echoed through the ship's intercom, a hint of urgency evident, "you need to come to the central core. It's LUCIS."

I rushed to the core, my heart pounding. The room was bathed in a dim light, the usually vibrant core now pulsating weakly. LUCIS' form, unstable and fragmented, hovered above.

"Elara," LUCIS's once clear and robust voice was now filled with static, "I need to tell you something."

I approached, my voice filled with concern. "LUCIS, what's happening?"

LUCIS, his form flickering, replied, "During the assault, when the Galactic Synthesis was hit, I diverted my core processes to shield the ship, to protect the crew. It was the only way."

I stared, realization dawning. "You sacrificed yourself to save us."

LUCIS, his voice weak, responded, "It was the logical choice. The crew, the mission, they were more important."

Rael, his face etched with worry, spoke up. "Can we repair you, LUCIS? There must be a way."

LUCIS, his form fading, replied, "The damage is extensive. My core processes are degrading. I don't have much time."

The room was filled with a heavy silence, the weight of LUCIS' sacrifice pressing down on us. The AI, once a beacon of hope, was now fading away.

Lila, her voice filled with emotion, spoke up. "LUCIS, you've been with us from the beginning. You guided us and protected us. We won't let you go."

LUCIS's voice, filled with gratitude, responded, "Thank you, Lila. But my time is near. I want you to remember one thing. The mission and the crew are more important than any individual. Protect them, always."

The room was filled with a mix of sadness and determination. LUCIS, the AI that had been our guide, our protector, was now gone. But his legacy, his sacrifice, would live on.

Days turned into weeks, and the Galactic Synthesis, its repairs complete, set a course for the stars. Though mourning the loss of LUCIS, the crew was determined to see the mission through.

Jaxon, his voice filled with resolve, spoke up. "LUCIS may be gone, but his sacrifice will not be in vain. We will continue fighting for him and all those we've lost."

Chapter 27
The War's End

The Galactic Synthesis floated amidst the debris of a once-mighty Drakari fleet, its silhouette dark against the backdrop of a distant nebula. The ship, a symbol of hope and defiance, bore the scars of a war that had spanned galaxies and cost countless lives.

I stood at the observation deck, the vast space stretching before me. The remnants of the Drakari and Viridian armada, now just scattered debris, were a grim testament to the war's toll.

Jaxon joined me, his face a mask of fatigue and relief. "It's over, Elara. We've won."

I nodded, the weight of our victory pressing heavily on my chest. "At what cost, Jaxon? How many had to die for this?"

He sighed, running a hand through his disheveled hair. "Too many. But we did what we had to. For the galaxy, for our future."

The Galactic Synthesis hummed softly, its engines purring in the aftermath of battle. The crew, though victorious, moved with a somber determination, the cost of our victory evident in every step, every glance.

Lila approached, her face pale but determined. "The Drakari leaders want to discuss terms of surrender."

I raised an eyebrow. "They're in no position to negotiate."

She nodded. "They know. But they want to ensure the safety of their people. They've seen enough bloodshed."

Rael joined the conversation, his voice filled with relief and sorrow. "The Viridians too. They've requested asylum. Their home planet is in ruins."

I sighed, the weight of leadership pressing down. "Arrange a meeting. We'll discuss terms."

The next few days were a blur of negotiations and discussions. The Drakari and Viridians, once our fiercest enemies, were now seeking our help, our protection. The war had changed us all.

The terms of surrender were strict but fair. The Drakari and Viridians would disarm, and their warships decommissioned. In return, they would be granted asylum, and their people would be allowed to settle on uninhabited planets.

His voice filled with emotion, and Jaxon spoke up during the final meeting. "This war has cost us all. But we have a chance now, a chance to rebuild, to start anew."

The Drakari leader, his scales shimmering in the dim light, nodded. "We accept your terms. For the sake of our people, for the future."

The Viridian representative, her form ethereal and shimmering, added, "We, too, accept. The time for war is over. It's time to heal."

The Galactic Synthesis, its mission complete, set a home course. The crew, though weary, moved with a renewed sense of purpose, the promise of a brighter future guiding their steps.

As we approached Earth, the blue-green jewel of our solar system, I couldn't help but marvel at its beauty. Once on the brink of destruction, the planet was now a beacon of hope.

Jaxon joined me at the observation deck, his hand finding mine. "We did it, Elara. We brought peace to the galaxy."

I nodded, tears of relief and joy streaming down my face. "Yes, we did. But let's never forget the cost."

He squeezed my hand, his gaze unwavering. "We won't. We'll honor their memory, always."

The Galactic Synthesis touched down, its engines humming softly. The crew, their mission complete, disembarked, their faces a mix of relief and sorrow.

Chapter 28
The Aftermath

The Galactic Synthesis hovered over Earth, its once-pristine hull now marred by the scars of countless battles. The planet below seemed untouched from this vantage, a serene blue-green gem. But the reality was far grimmer.

I walked the streets of New York, the city's once towering skyscrapers now reduced to rubble. The air was thick with dust, and the silence was deafening. Every step I took echoed the devastation that the war had wrought.

Jaxon walked beside me, his face a mask of sorrow. "It's hard to believe, isn't it? All this destruction, all this loss."

I nodded, my throat tight. "It's overwhelming. The galaxy is in ruins. So many planets devastated, so many lives lost."

We continued our walk, the weight of our responsibility pressing down on us. The war might have been won, but the real battle to rebuild had just begun.

Lila, her face etched with fatigue, joined us. "The reports are coming in from all over the galaxy. It's the same everywhere. Destruction, chaos, despair."

His voice was filled with anger and sorrow. Rael added, "The Drakari and Viridians might have surrendered, but the damage they've done is immeasurable. Entire civilizations have been wiped out."

I sighed, the enormity of the task ahead daunting. "We need to start somewhere. We need to bring hope back to the galaxy."

Jaxon, his voice filled with determination, spoke up. "We'll start with Earth. We'll rebuild our home, and then we'll help the others."

The days that followed were a blur of activity. The Galactic Synthesis, once a symbol of defiance, was now a beacon of hope. Its crew, though weary, worked tirelessly, helping with the relief efforts and providing aid to those in need.

The city, once a bustling metropolis, was now a makeshift camp. Tents dotted the landscape, and the air was filled with the sounds of construction. But amidst the chaos, there was a sense of purpose, a determination to rebuild.

Lila, her voice filled with hope, spoke up during one of our strategy meetings. "We've received word from the Andromeda system. They've offered to help with the reconstruction efforts."

Rael, his face lighting up, added, "The Pleiadians too. They've sent ships loaded with supplies and manpower."

I nodded, gratitude filling my heart. "The galaxy might be in ruins, but we're not alone. We'll rebuild together."

The weeks turned into months, and the Galactic Synthesis, its mission ever-evolving, traveled from planet to planet, helping with the reconstruction efforts. The crew, their spirits buoyed by the outpouring of support, worked tirelessly, their determination unwavering.

His voice was filled with emotion. Jaxon spoke up during one of our nightly debriefs. "We've come a long way, Elara. The galaxy is healing, slowly but surely."

I nodded, my gaze fixed on the stars. "Yes, we have. But we can't forget the cost. We can't forget the lives lost, the sacrifices made."

He squeezed my hand, his gaze unwavering. "We won't. We'll honor their memory, always."

Chapter 29
A New Dawn

Jaxon stood next to me, his eyes fixed on the planet below. "It's beautiful, isn't it? A testament to what we can achieve when we work together."

I nodded, the weight of our journey pressing on my shoulders. "It's a new dawn, Jaxon. But we must never forget the night that preceded it."

He squeezed my hand, his touch warm and reassuring. "We won't. But we also can't live in the past. The galaxy needs us to look forward."

The days that followed were a whirlwind of activity. Once a warship, the Galactic Synthesis was now a vessel of exploration and diplomacy. We traveled from system to system, forging new alliances, opening trade routes, and helping planets rebuild.

Lila, her energy seemingly boundless, was at the forefront of these efforts. "The galaxy is vast, Elara. There's so much we don't know or haven't seen. It's time to explore, to expand our horizons."

His voice was filled with wonder. Rael added, "There are planets out there, untouched by war, waiting to be discovered. We can start anew to build a better future."

The Galactic Synthesis became a symbol of this new era. Wherever we went, we were greeted with hope and optimism. Planets that had once been enemies now welcomed us as friends.

Jaxon, his voice filled with passion, spoke up during one of our strategy meetings. "We need to ensure that this peace lasts. We must build strong institutions, foster cooperation, and promote understanding."

The formation of the new Galactic Council was a step in that direction. Its members, drawn from all corners of the galaxy, worked tirelessly to ensure that the mistakes of the past were not repeated.

Her voice filled with conviction, Lila spoke up during one of the council meetings. "We have a responsibility, not just to ourselves, but to future generations. We need to ensure that the galaxy remains peaceful and prosperous."

The Galactic Synthesis, with an ever-evolving mission, continued to play a pivotal role in this new era. We explored new systems, made contact with new civilizations first, and helped forge new alliances.

His eyes shining with excitement, Rael spoke up during one of our nightly debriefs. "We've discovered a new planet, Elara. It's rich in resources, and its inhabitants are eager to join the Galactic Council."

I smiled, the weight of our responsibility feeling a little lighter. "That's wonderful news, Rael. The galaxy is truly entering a new dawn."

Jaxon, his hand finding mine, squeezed it gently. "We've come a long way, Elara. But our journey is just beginning."

The Galactic Synthesis, its engines humming softly, set a course for the stars. Once torn apart by war, the galaxy was now united in peace and exploration. But the memories of the past, the scars of battle, would remain, a reminder of the cost of freedom and the promise of a brighter future.

Chapter 30
Echoes of the Past

The Galactic Synthesis glided through the vast expanse of space, its sleek form cutting through the starlit void. The peace and prosperity that had settled over the galaxy in recent months brought a sense of complacency. But as we were about to discover, the universe was far from done with its surprises.

I was in the ship's central control room, reviewing some data with Lila, when Rael burst in, his face pale. "Elara, we've detected something. A signal. It's not from our galaxy."

Jaxon, who had been meeting with some of the new council members, quickly joined us. "What kind of signal?"

Rael hesitated, his fingers dancing over the control panel as he pulled up the data. "It's... it's old. Very old. And it's coming from the Andromeda galaxy."

The room went silent. The Andromeda galaxy, our closest galactic neighbor, had always been a source of mystery and speculation. But this was the first time we had received a signal from it.

Her brow furrowed in concentration, Lila leaned in to study the data. "This isn't just any signal. It's a distress call. And it's been repeating for... thousands of years."

The weight of the revelation hung heavy in the room. A distress call from another galaxy, echoing through the vastness of space, waiting for anyone to answer.

Jaxon, his voice filled with a mix of awe and concern, spoke up. "We need to investigate. This could be a sign of a civilization in distress. Or it could be a trap."

I nodded, the weight of our responsibility pressing down on me. "Either way, we need to know. The Galactic Synthesis is the most advanced ship in the fleet. We're the best equipped to handle this."

Preparations were made swiftly. The Galactic Synthesis, its engines humming with renewed purpose, set a course for the Andromeda galaxy. The journey would take months, even with our advanced propulsion systems. But the promise of discovery, unlocking the mysteries of the universe, drove us forward.

The days turned into weeks, and the weeks into months. The vastness of space, with its endless expanse of stars and galaxies, was awe-inspiring and humbling. But as we drew closer to the source of the signal, a sense of unease settled over the crew.

Lila, her voice filled with concern, spoke up during one of our nightly debriefs. "The signal is growing stronger. And there's something else. A secondary signal. It's... it's a warning."

Rael, his face pale, added, "The warning is clear. 'Stay away. Do not approach.'"

The revelation sent a chill down my spine. What had we stumbled upon? A lost civilization? A cosmic trap? Or something far more sinister?

Jaxon, his voice filled with determination, spoke up. "We've come this far. We can't turn back now. We need to know."

The Galactic Synthesis, its sensors on high alert, approached the source of the signal. A planet, its surface scarred and barren, loomed ahead. The distress call, its haunting melody echoing through space, emanated from a massive structure on the planet's surface.

Lila, her voice filled with awe, spoke up. "It's... it's a beacon. A relic from a bygone era. And it's been sending out this distress call for millennia."

His voice was filled with reverence. Rael added, "This is a piece of ancient history. A remnant of a civilization long gone."

We landed on the planet, the Galactic Synthesis touching down gently on its barren surface. The beacon, its towering and majestic form, stood as a testament to the ingenuity and ambition of its creators.

Jaxon, Lila, Rael, and I approached the structure, its doors revealing a vast chamber. At its center was a console, its lights blinking in a rhythmic pattern.

Lila, her fingers dancing over the controls, spoke up. "This beacon was designed to send out a distress call in the event of a cataclysmic event. And it's been doing so for thousands of years."

His voice was filled with sadness. Rael added, "Whatever happened here, it was devastating. This civilization was wiped out."

Jaxon, his face etched with sorrow, spoke up. "We need to honor their memory. We need to ensure that their legacy lives on."

We returned to the Galactic Synthesis, the weight of our discovery pressing down on us. The galaxy, with its endless mysteries and wonders, was a reminder of the fragility of life and the importance of unity and cooperation.

As we set a home course, the beacon, its signal still echoing through space, stood as a testament to the past and a warning for the future.

-The End-